PRODIGIES UNLEASHED

Crown Jewels Vol II

M S DHONI GLOBAL SCHOOL

ISBN

Hardcase 979-8-89632-759-2
Paperback 979-8-89610-992-1

This book has been published with all efforts taken to make the material error-free after the consent of the author. However, the author and the publisher do not assume and hereby disclaim any liability to any party for any loss, damage, or disruption caused by errors or omissions, whether such errors or omissions result from negligence, accident, or any other cause.

While every effort has been made to avoid any mistake or omission, this publication is being sold on the condition and understanding that neither the author nor the publishers or printers would be liable in any manner to any person by reason of any mistake or omission in this publication or for any action taken or omitted to be taken or advice rendered or accepted on the basis of this work. For any defect in printing or binding the publishers will be liable only to replace the defective copy by another copy of this work then available.

CONTENTS

FOREWORD BY MR. MS DHONI

It brings me great pride and joy to introduce *Prodigies Unleashed – Crown Jewels Vol II & Vol III*, a testament to the immense talent and creativity cultivated at M S Dhoni Global School. In our journey to provide a holistic and forward-thinking education, this anthology stands as a milestone, showcasing the voices of our young authors from the Hosur and Bangalore campuses.

Just as cricket requires both individual dedication and teamwork, storytelling too involves a blend of personal insight and the guidance of mentors. Through these stories, I see the students' unique perspectives come to life, reflecting their courage, imagination, and curiosity about the world. Their work inspires not only the readers but also a generation of students who, through such platforms, realize that their ideas are valuable and impactful.

This compilation of stories celebrates the determination of each student to express themselves and take pride in their creativity. As they embrace storytelling, they take steps toward becoming confident communicators and thoughtful leaders—qualities that will serve them well in all their future pursuits. This book, in essence, is a celebration of their journey, one that I am honoured to support.

My heartiest congratulations to the students and faculty of M S Dhoni Global School. As you turn these pages, may you be inspired by the creativity and courage displayed here, knowing that this is just the beginning for these talented authors.

Yours,

MS Dhoni

FOREWORD
BY DR. KANNAN GIREESH

It gives me immense pleasure to write the foreword for Prodigies Unleashed – Crown Jewels Vol II & Vol III, a compilation that not only celebrates the creativity and imagination of the students at M S Dhoni Global School but also aligns with the values we hold dear through the Leader in Me program.

As a firm believer in the power of education to shape the leaders of tomorrow, I see this anthology as a testament to the incredible potential of our young minds. The stories shared in these pages reflect the diversity of thought, vision, and expression that define the students of the Hosur and Bangalore campuses. They have woven tales from different genres—adventure, mystery, fantasy, and drama—giving us a glimpse into their boundless creativity and an insight into how they view the world around them.

At Live Life Education, we are committed to nurturing leaders who are not only academically competent but also emotionally intelligent, socially responsible, and compassionate. This anthology, while showcasing the imaginative works of our students, also serves as an inspiration to them. It teaches them that leadership begins with self-expression, the courage to share one's ideas, and the ability to grow through every experience.

What stands out in this collection is the authenticity and honesty with which these young authors have shared their stories. These works are a reminder that creativity is a muscle that must be exercised, and through such platforms, we are equipping our students with the tools they need to become confident communicators and thoughtful leaders.

I am proud of the students for embracing this opportunity to express themselves and for the mentors who have guided them in their journey. Congratulations to the students of M S Dhoni Global School for their outstanding work. I look forward to witnessing your continued growth and success as writers, thinkers, and leaders of tomorrow.

Sincerely,

Dr. Kannan Gireesh
Founder, Live Life Education

FOREWORD
BY MR. BHAVIN SHAH

It is a true privilege to contribute the foreword to Prodigies Unleashed – Crown Jewels Vol II & Vol III, a reflection of the boundless creativity fostered at M S Dhoni Global School. This school has long championed an educational vision that combines rigorous academics with platforms for personal growth, cultivating an environment where students are inspired to pursue their creative and intellectual passions.

This anthology exemplifies that vision, bringing together stories across genres—from mystery and adventure to heartfelt drama. It highlights the unique voices of students from the Hosur and Bangalore campuses and celebrates their journey as budding authors, offering readers a genuine glimpse into their imaginations.

Through works like this, M S Dhoni Global School empowers students to explore new ideas, communicate effectively, and understand the transformative power of storytelling. It's my hope that this book will not only inspire its readers but also remind these young authors of the importance of curiosity, resilience, and self-expression on their journey to becoming the next generation of thinkers and leaders.

Congratulations to the students and mentors who have dedicated themselves to this project. May Prodigies Unleashed be the first step of many as you continue your journey of growth and achievement.

Regards,

Mr. Bhavin Shah
CEO & Director, EducationWorld

PREFACE

Prodigies Unleashed – Crown Jewels Vol II & Vol III is a celebration of creativity, imagination, and the potential of the young minds at M S Dhoni Global School. This collection, featuring the voices of students from both the Hosur (Vol II) and Bangalore (Vol III) campuses, brings together a range of stories that explore various genres—from adventure and mystery to fantasy and heartfelt drama.

Each story in this anthology represents a unique perspective, a glimpse into the thoughts and dreams of students who are beginning their journey as writers. This compilation is not about perfection; it is about growth, learning, and discovery. By giving our students a platform to express themselves, we hope to encourage them to explore their creativity, understand the power of storytelling, and develop their voices as authors.

Through this book, we aim to foster the values of leadership, resilience, and self-expression, helping our students realize that their creativity is a valuable asset in becoming leaders not only in their chosen fields but also in their communities. This anthology serves as a stepping stone, motivating our young writers to continue developing their skills and confidence, paving the way for a future where their stories will continue to inspire and lead.

We are proud of our students for taking the first steps in their literary journey. This anthology is a reflection of their hard work, imagination, and determination. May it serve as a reminder that the path to greatness begins with a single word, a single story, and a single dream.

ACKNOWLEDGMENT

Ideas transform into reality through collective effort, inspiration, and unwavering support. As we unveil *Prodigies Unleashed – Crown Jewels Vol II*, we take a moment to reflect on the journey that brought this book to life and express our heartfelt gratitude to those who made it possible.

At the forefront of this endeavour is our school mentor, Mr. Mahendra Singh Dhoni, an inspiration to millions of youth in India and around the world. His remarkable career and commitment to excellence are a testament to the values we instill at M S Dhoni Global School. Our students have had the unparalleled privilege of engaging closely with him as a mentor. His campus visit, where he interacted personally with every student, left a lasting impact, motivating them to dream big and persevere. His foreword for this anthology beautifully reflects his encouragement for students to embrace creativity as a stepping stone toward leadership and self-expression.

We are equally honoured to have the continued association of Dr. Kannan Gireesh and Mr. Bhavin Shah, close acquaintances of our school for many years. Our sincere thanks also extend to Dr. Kannan Gireesh, a renowned psychiatrist, psychotherapist, and founder of Live Life

Education. His foreword highlights the role of creativity in leadership and personal development. Dr. Gireesh's commitment to holistic education aligns perfectly with the values we aim to instill in our students.

We are privileged to feature the insights of Mr. Bhavin Shah, CEO, and Director of EducationWorld, whose foreword celebrates the transformative power of storytelling. A pioneer in educational thought leadership, his encouragement motivates us to create platforms where students can express themselves fearlessly and explore their intellectual horizons.

This journey would not have been possible without the invaluable support of the school management. Our deepest gratitude goes to Mr. Chandrasekar, Chairman; Mrs. Bhuvaneswari Chandrasekar, Senior Principal and Correspondent; Mr. Vineeth Chandrasekar, Vice-Chairman & Director (Admin & Operations); Mrs. Deepitha, Director (HR); Mr. Vishnu Gaurav Selvaraj, Director (IT & Sports); and Mrs. Nikitha, Director (Admissions & Onboarding). Their vision and encouragement were instrumental in creating this platform for students to showcase their creativity.

We extend heartfelt thanks to the school principals, Mrs. Hema Malini and Mrs. Gayathri, for their relentless support and belief in the potential of this project. The commitment of the Coordinators, the teachers, and the Design and Technical team ensured this book reached the highest standards of quality and creativity.

A special acknowledgment is extended to the exceptional members of our English Team who were directly involved in the meticulous process of compiling and refining this anthology. Their relentless dedication and collaborative effort have been pivotal in transforming this vision into reality. We sincerely appreciate the hard work of Mrs. Felcita Fernandez, Mrs. Vandana Singh G, Ms. Divya Christy S, Ms. Faaiza Nidha C, Ms. Jenifer E, Mrs. Kavinela Sakthi, Mrs. Kavya M, Mrs. R Anandhapriya, Mrs. Aparna Raju, Mrs. Prajila VV, Ms. Sweety Infanta S, Mrs. Kasturi P, Mrs. Saranya Thirumoorthi, Mrs. Vaishnavi B, Ms. Bhuvaneshwari R, Mrs. Netra Devi Manivannan, Mrs. Ghayathri Murugan, Mr. Suresh Govindhappa, Mrs. Krishnaveni K P, Mr. Yonas M, and myself, Mrs. Farzana A, for their significant contributions.

Finally, we extend our heartfelt congratulations to the young authors whose creativity and hard work have brought this book to life. Each story is a testament to their imagination and dedication. As a team, we are proud to celebrate their journey and look forward to seeing their talents flourish in the years to come.

01

AUREA TERRA

– SUBASREE LEKSHMANAN

In the inspiring city of New York, there were three friends-Liz, Claire, and Miranda. They were the best of friends anyone could ever think of. Due to the exceptional interest, she had in playing the guitar, Liz's parents had agreed to transfer her to Hampton Middle School, where all students were allowed to be trained to play an instrument of their choice. However, Liz missed her friends a great deal. So, after many calls, they'd finalized a date for a get-together at Liz's house. When Claire and Miranda, arrived, the three of them wanted to play a game of Monopoly. Liz remembered that her old monopoly board was in the attic and went to fetch it. Several minutes passed, but Liz hadn't returned yet. So, her friends went to the attic of their house to look for her. There, they found her trying to open what appeared to be an old box. When Liz saw them arrive, she said, 'Guys, look at this. I've never seen this before. It was in the corner of the attic. I found it while searching for my monopoly board.' She showed them the box. Claire, who was extremely interested in anything that belonged to the past, came closer and looked at the box curiously. 'Look at this,' she said examining the box closely. 'A.A'

'What can that mean?' Asked Miranda

'Was there anyone in your family who had these initials?' Claire asked Liz.

'Hang on. Let me think.' Said Liz.

After some time, Liz said excitedly, 'Yes, yes, there was a person in my family having these initials. My great-great-grandfather, Alexander Antilles.'

'Hmmm… Let's see,' said Claire. 'Was he known for anything? Recognized for something, probably?'

'Yes,' said Liz. 'He was a scientist.'

'The matter is, how are we going to open this box?' Said Claire.

'Hang on,' said Miranda. 'I have a pen knife with me. You can try to force one lock with it. It's strong.'

They tried and somehow managed to force open the lock of the old chest with Miranda's pen knife.

Inside, there appeared to be two old pieces of parchment. One appeared to be a map while the other was a drawing of some sort.

Miranda picked the map up. 'This looks like the map of our city.' She spoke.

They noticed that a cross was marked on the place where the current 'New York World of Science' was located and the words 'Perdita', 'degree', and 'Ianuae' were written. And something that looked like a capsule was also there.

Miranda, who was bright in Latin said, 'Perdita, means lost, degree means rediscover and lane means teleport.'

'There must be something there that your grandfather wanted us to rediscover.' Said Claire. 'Something that was lost and can be found by teleportation, probably?'

So, they decided to go to the New York Hall of Science.

There, they went straight to the space section because the first thing they could relate to when they heard the term teleport was space.

After searching around for a while, they found something that resembled the capsule they'd found in the box. Below it, they saw the words 'Invented by Alexander Antilles, the teleportation capsule is believed to have the power to transfer or teleport human beings from Earth to Space and vice-versa. However, the usage of this capsule has not been possible to date.'

The trio of friends was probably the most excited group of people after reading the note.

They went home and researched more on the usage of the capsule. Due to the fact that there wasn't more information about the teleportation capsule, they had to try various methods on how to use the capsule. They had a rough idea of what needed to be done. They decided to try it out at night. So, when it was dark, the trio went to a large ground. The top of the capsule had a knob-like structure on it. They pulled it upwards, and the capsule became quite big. Then, they pressed a button on the side of the capsule, and it grew even more. It was enough for 5 people to get in. The three friends stepped in. Inside was everything a person could need to go to space - spacesuits, oxygen tanks, and communication devices. They wore spacesuits and prepared themselves for an adventure.

They pressed a button inside the capsule and saw a huge golden ring appear above them. The location was set to 'Aurea Terra' which, according to Miranda, was supposed to mean 'golden land'. They pressed a red button in the capsule and suddenly felt a jerk. They felt as if they were being pulled into the capsule. The three of them held hands and closed their eyes. If their calculation was correct, in 5 seconds, they were supposed to be in the 'area terra'. When they opened their eyes, they saw a whole new world. It was beautiful. It seemed as if the golden land was a huge canvas with a beautiful picture painted on it. They got out of the capsule and stepped onto the land. As they'd expected, the gravity was not the same. A light touch with their foot seemed enough to make them float. They broke a small piece of the ground from the golden land. Liz slowly removed her spacesuit. Nothing happened! Further explorations led to discoveries of possibilities of the existence of life there. They found water, and they were able to breathe, they just needed to adjust to the gravity, and all was set. They hurried back inside the capsule, and it once more took them back to Earth, they let the space scientists know about this spectacular discovery of theirs. Soon, further explorations were made and man started to migrate from Earth to the 'Aurea Terra'. The trio hoped that their future generations would live their life in the world discovered by them. After all, lost worlds are always rediscovered.

Author's Profile:

Subasree LS (Grade X) is an aspiring biostatistician with a deep passion for blending science with creativity. Known for her exceptional academic achievements, she is dedicated to advancing her knowledge in the field of biostatistics while nurturing a wide array of personal interests. In her spare time, Subasree enjoys reading fictional books, where she finds solace and inspiration. A keen chess player, she thrives on the intellectual challenge and strategic thinking that the game demands.

In addition to her academic and intellectual pursuits, Subasree is a gifted orator, captivating the audience with her eloquence and clarity of expression. Her talents extend to the arts as well, where she shines as a singer and artist, demonstrating a unique balance between analytical precision and creative flair. With her drive and diverse skill set, Subasree is on a promising path to make significant contributions through her writings as well.

02

THE HOLIDAYS

– DUSHYANTH S

In 2018, I went to my native place to see my grandparents. It was my first visit there. I was so happy that I met my grandparents. My grandfather told me to clean the garage. I started clearing out the metal things first. I noticed a box that said "Memories. "I thought it was just a box, and I kept it aside and started cleaning the garage again. It was 4 p.m. in the evening when I finished my work. I remembered the box, which I noticed earlier in the morning. When I opened the box; there were my grandparents' old pictures, engagement photos, and a note that said, "Go to the attic to find more information." I was so curious about what would be in the attic.

I went inside the house and asked my grandparents, where is the attic? My grandfather told me it was upstairs. I quickly went upstairs and opened the door. I saw a big picture of my grandparents, my parents, and 2 months old me. I explored even deeper; I saw a picture of my sister, who passed away when I was 1 year old. I cried aloud, and my grandparents rushed and tried to stop me from crying. They called my parents, who were returning to my place, and they said we would come back and stay there for a week. They came, and

I stopped crying and asked about my sister. They told me everything about my sister. We stayed about 2 days while sleeping. I had a dream about my sister and me playing happily in the garden. And just like that, 5 days passed. We went back home, and my heart reminded me of the picture.

Author's Profile:

Dushyanth S of grade V is an intelligent and knowledgeable Grade V student with a keen eye for observation. He shows a natural curiosity and enthusiasm for learning, often demonstrating a deep understanding. He is a thoughtful and introspective student who demonstrates a deep emotional awareness in his work.

03

EVE'S MAGICAL ADVENTURE

– KRUTIKA R

Once upon a time, a girl named Eve was sitting under a tree and reading a book. Suddenly, she fell asleep and saw a squirrel. She followed it, and the squirrel went climbing up a tree. She climbed too and saw it waving at her, so she waved back. The squirrel smiled and went down the tree.

She looked down and suddenly fell into a hole. She found a door, but it was too small for her to fit through. Then, a cake appeared out of nowhere that could talk. The cake told her to "Eat me!" and said it would make her smaller so she could fit through the door. She ate the cake, became tiny, and went inside and continued walking through a world of candy and sweets. She took a bite and was amazed by the delicious, rich, chocolatey flavours. Her eyes filled with joy! After taking several bites, she saw a woman walking with a crowd she felt suspicious.

She asked, "Who are you?" and the woman, who turned out to be the queen of this land, answered rudely, accusing Eve of taking a bite of her chocolates and sweets. The queen threatened to have her guards kill her. Despite the queen's rudeness, Eve remained polite, and the queen invited her to the castle.

When they arrived, the queen was prepared to have her executed. Terrified, Eve ran away and stumbled upon another queen, who was very kind. This kind queen apologized to Eve, feeling it was her fault for not warning her about the evil queen.

Eve asked if she would go to war against the evil queen, and the kind queen agreed. They went to confront the evil queen, who accepted the challenge. The next morning, both queens' armies were ready for battle. The war began, and the kind queen won.

Everyone celebrated, but then Eve saw everything fading away. She soon realized she had been dreaming. Her sister arrived just in time to call her for dinner. Eve went with her sister and shared her incredible experience with her family, including her mother, father, and sister. They all enjoyed the meal together.

Author's Profile:

Krutika from grade V is an active and extraordinary artist, known for her exceptional talent in drawing. She is diligent in her work, consistently performing her tasks with care and precision. Krutika's command of language is commendable, and her energetic spirit makes her a valuable team player, always ready to support and inspire her classmates.

04

THE MYSTERIOUS FOREST

– MOWLINI B

Once upon a time, there was a mysterious forest. People believed only the brave could enter this forest. But one day, a boy and a girl named Danush and Sruthi, though a little afraid, packed their bags and set off on a journey to explore it. As they entered, a voice echoed, saying, "Once you enter, you cannot leave until you pass all the tests and overcome the obstacles inside." Undeterred, they were ready to face any challenge.

They stepped through the door, and the forest was indeed mysterious and spooky. Their first challenge appeared in the form of three doors, one of which would lead them to a treasure. However, they chose the wrong door, entering a mystery filled with lessons on kindness and honesty. Each time they solved a puzzle, another would appear, never seeming to end. As night fell, they took out a pillow and blanket from their bags and went to sleep.

The next day, they resumed their journey. Sruthi realized that they had taken the wrong door and couldn't go back. Determined to find a solution, they consulted a book they had brought, hoping it would help them navigate the maze.

They analyzed the three doors, trying to figure out which one led to the treasure, and set off once more toward the correct door.

Just as they were about to enter, a voice said, "You will receive the treasure not only for finding it but also for your kindness to others." They remembered the help they had given to people along their journey, and with brave hearts, they stepped inside, only to be greeted by a stunningly beautiful natural landscape.

However, the puzzles grew harder than they had anticipated. Through teamwork and determination, they overcame each puzzle that stood in their way.

Finally, they reached the treasure, but they couldn't enter the gate because the God of Treasure needed to grant them permission. As they waited, the voice announced that the God of Treasure would arrive the next day. They read some books, ate, and slept peacefully.

In the morning, the God of Treasure appeared and said, "You have worked as a team and reached this point, but only one of you can endure the final trial. Decide among yourselves." Danush and Sruthi didn't argue over the treasure. Instead, they suggested that the God of Treasure split it between them, as they both valued fairness and friendship.

MORAL: We should not fight over possessions. Instead, we should be willing to share, always speak the truth, and show kindness and honesty toward others.

Author's Profile:

Mowlini of grade V is a talented student who stands out for her skills in various areas. Whether it's academics, arts, or problem-solving, she demonstrates an ability to excel and adapt. Mowlini approaches tasks with focus and determination, and her talent allows her to quickly master new concepts

05

WHISPERS OF THE FOREST

– SANA.M

In the heart of the ancient Eden Wood Forest, many whispered that a legend thrived in a hidden glen where time stood still and magic whispered through the trees. Although many sought it, only a few returned, their stories filled with either wonder or madness. Among those enchanted by the tales was a young girl named Lila, whose curiosity often led her into trouble.

One crisp autumn morning, with leaves crunching underfoot, Lila decided to venture deeper into the woods than ever before. Armed with nothing but her sense of adventure and a small satchel of bread, she followed a narrow path that wound like a serpent through the towering pines. As the sun filtered through the branches, painting the ground with dappled light, she felt an inexplicable pull guiding her forward.

After hours of wandering, she stumbled upon a clearing bathed in ethereal light. At its center stood an enormous oak tree, its gnarled branches stretching towards the sky. The air shimmered with an otherworldly energy, and Lila could hear faint whispers, like a lullaby drifting on the wind. Intrigued, she approached the tree, running her fingers along its tough bark.

Soon enough, she could hear a voice calling out to her, whispering, "Lila, Lila, come here." The voice then added, "Welcome, seeker." Scared and surprised, Lila asked, "Who are you?" "I am the Guardian of the Glen," replied the voice. Seeing Lila shiver, the Guardian added, "If you stay here, you will see your dreams and memories intertwine."

Lila hesitated but eventually agreed. Then, a mist of smoke surrounded her, but there was a clear image. She watched herself as a child, laughing with her friends by the river. Suddenly, the atmosphere turned heavy, as if even the wind felt sorrowful when she saw the day she lost her dog. A shadow of sadness crept into her heart, and an eerie stillness filled the air.

Wanting to help Lila overcome her sorrow, a beautiful woman appeared. Her hands were adorned with golden bracelets, and her neck was decorated with hundreds of pearls. She was dressed as if even the moon could not challenge her charm.

The woman introduced herself, saying, "Hello, Lila. I am the Guardian of the Forest."

Wanting Lila to smile and feel the warmth of the Glen, the Guardian touched her shoulder and whispered in her ear, "To find joy, you must embrace even the dark."

With tears in her eyes, Lila whispered, "I don't want to remember the pain."

Seeing Lila in a state of sorrow, the Guardian began chanting spells, showing the enchanting beauty of the Glen. As the cloud of smoke faded, Lila soon realized that she could honour her past without letting it define her. Wiping away her tears, Lila hugged the woman and said, "Thank you so much."

From that day on, Lila visited the Glen and the Guardian often. Every time she did, memories flooded her heart, but they were now filled with a sense of magic and acceptance.

Author's Profile:

Sana.M, a grade VII student, is an avid reader with a deep love for fantasy books, often getting lost in magical worlds and epic adventures. Her passion for storytelling is reflected in her impressive stage speeches, which have earned her widespread admiration for her confidence, clarity, and engaging delivery. She is also known for her ability to weave imaginative narratives that captivate her audience, making her a natural communicator both on and off stage.

06

THE CASE OF THE MISSING KEY

– SAI RISHITHA T

It was a rainy evening when Lyla noticed something unusual: her front door key, usually resting in the small dish by the window, was mysteriously missing. Living alone in her cottage on the edge of town, she wasn't one to misplace things, which only heightened her concern. Frowning, she began to retrace her steps from that morning, hoping to uncover the key's whereabouts. As she pondered her next move, she decided to enlist the help of James, her neighbour, and a local locksmith. With his expertise, they would search high and low, and together, they would unravel the mystery behind the key's disappearance. What secrets could be lurking just around the corner?

"Odd," James exclaimed, adjusting his spectacles as a shiver of intrigue swept through the room. "Are you certain no one else has set foot in here?"

Lyla's heart raced as she shook her head, determination shining in her eyes. "Not a soul."

Just then, a memory flared to life in her mind: Oliver, her mischievous cat, had been acting peculiar all day. An instinct tugged at her. Dropping to her knees, she glanced under the sofa where Oliver often hid his secrets. Among a cluster of shiny treasures and a weathered toy mouse, there it was—her missing key!

With a triumphant laugh, she turned to James. "Looks like our little thief has been unmasked!"

James grinned, his eyes twinkling with delight. "You know, it's always the smallest suspects that hold the biggest surprises, Lyla."

Outside, the rain drummed a relentless beat against the window, but inside, a thrilling sense of victory enveloped Lyla.

James smiled warmly. "Always check the smallest suspects first, Lyla."

The rain continued to patter outside, but inside, Lyla felt a sense of calm. The mystery was solved, and there was no trace of danger—only a bit of feline mischief.

Author's Profile:

Sai Rishitha (Grade VIII), a creative young writer, is the author of The Case of the Missing Key. Her story combines mystery and intrigue, drawing readers into a suspenseful plot filled with clever clues and unexpected twists. Sai's writing showcases her keen observation skills and her talent for creating engaging, thought-provoking narratives. Her storytelling reflects a passion for unraveling mysteries and capturing readers' imaginations.

07

THE TWO EXPLORERS

– SAI AARUSH A

Mr. Nick (Old Bunny and Strawberry's Grandpa) - Owner of the Magical Castle

Molang (Bunny No.1) - Kind and Helpful

Strawberry (Bunny No.2) - Courageous and Brave

"Hey! Molang, Strawberry. Come here; I want to share something with you about my magical castle," said Mr. Nick.

"Yes, Grandpa, we are eager to listen," said Molang and Strawberry.

"There is a castle that was owned by my ancestors, and now I am the one who owns it. The way to the castle is through a small hole near the Food Production Industry. Inside the castle, there are four magical statues, each with an excellent natural power.

If you wish, you can take them with you and use them. However, since the castle is very old, it could collapse at any time. So, hurry up, go and explore, but be sure to come back safely," said Mr. Nick.

Molang and Strawberry were excited and began their journey to the castle. They ventured through the small hole and soon found themselves inside the castle, their hearts full of excitement. As they explored the castle, they discovered the four magical statues.

The first statue had the power of magnetic force, which could attract anything they wished. The second statue could provide an invisible defensive force field to protect them from enemies. The third statue had the power of quick and immediate healing. The fourth statue had the ability to stop any natural disaster.

Molang chose the third statue, and Strawberry took the remaining ones. Both of them used the magical powers of the statues to help their friends, but they never allowed anyone else to touch them.

A few days later, Molang visited Strawberry, only to find that Strawberry was extremely ill. Molang quickly hurried back to his home, took his statue, and used its healing power to heal Strawberry. Strawberry instantly felt better and looked healthy again.

Later, while Molang and Strawberry were playing hide and seek, suddenly a powerful F1 tornado appeared, and Molang was lifted into the air by the tornado. Although Strawberry panicked, she quickly grabbed all her statues.

First, she used the second statue to create an invisible force field, protecting herself from the tornado. Then, she used the first statue to attract Molang out of the tornado, and he safely landed on the ground. Finally, she used the fourth statue to stop the tornado, and once it was over, she deactivated the force field.

They both felt relieved and happy and continued playing together. Molang thanked Strawberry for saving him and admired her ability to stay calm and use her quick thinking even in such a panic-inducing situation.

MORAL: We should be kind, sharing, and grateful.

Author's Profile:

Sai Aarush (Grade IV) demonstrates exceptional talent across a wide range of subjects. He listens attentively to his teachers and peers, always showing consideration for others' opinions and feelings. His ability to empathize with others and think critically about situations makes him a compassionate and responsible individual.

08

THE ADVENTURE OF VIJAY ON TREASURE ISLAND

– SAI SHARVAN M

Once upon a time, there was a boy named Vijay who loved to explore. One day, he heard about an island named Treasure Island, which was rumored to hold a huge treasure. However, it was not easy to reach. Excited about the adventure, Vijay packed a backpack with food and began his journey to the island. After a long trip, he finally arrived and took a rest.

The next day, he started searching for the treasure but felt disappointed when he couldn't find it. The following day, as he continued his search, he suddenly heard a mysterious voice. The voice told him that to open the treasure, he needed to find four special diamonds: red, green, blue, and yellow. Each diamond represented a test:

- The red diamond would test his honesty.
- The green diamond would test his bravery.
- The blue diamond would test his kindness.
- The yellow diamond would test his strength.

The voice explained that once he put all these diamonds into the treasure box, it would unlock. Then, the voice faded, and Vijay found a map showing the locations of the diamonds and the treasure. The next day, he followed the map to the location of the red diamond. As he approached, the voice spoke again, saying, "If you pass the test of honesty, you will receive the red diamond." The voice asked, "Have you ever been punished by your mother?" Vijay honestly replied, "Yes." Because he answered truthfully, he received the red diamond.

Next, he traveled to the green diamond, where he was transported to a dark room. The voice said, "If you are brave, you will pass the test of bravery." Vijay stood his ground and passed the test, so he received the green diamond.

Then he moved on to the blue diamond, where he suddenly found himself as a babysitter. The voice instructed, "If you take good care of the children, you will pass the test of kindness." Vijay took care of the children well and earned the blue diamond.

Finally, he went to the yellow diamond. He was transported to a place where an arm-wrestling competition was taking place. The voice said, "If you win this arm-wrestling match, you will pass the test of strength." Vijay competed and won, successfully earning the yellow diamond.

With all four diamonds in hand, Vijay followed the map to the treasure box. He carefully set each diamond into its place on the box, and the treasure unlocked. Vijay had succeeded in his quest and obtained the treasure.

Author's Profile:

Sai Sharvan of grade V is a skilled and responsible student who demonstrates excellent leadership qualities in the classroom and beyond. He has a natural ability to take charge of situations, helping to guide his peers during group activities and ensuring tasks are completed efficiently. He is always polite, listens carefully to others, and shows a willingness to help those around him.

09

A NOBLE SOUL

– SUBASREE LEKSHMANAN

It was a beautiful morning in the city of Hillwood. Max was playing with his friends in a park nearby. They had caught a little puppy and were trying to force the frightened little creature to shake paws with them and perform some tricks. Max's grandfather was strolling down the street, and he happened to come across the park. He called the children and asked them,

'Children, why were you troubling the poor animal?', he asked.

'But, Grandpa, we were just trying to make it shake paws.', said Max.

'Forcing an animal to shake paws isn't right, son', said his grandfather.

'Do you all know the story of Princess Liz?', he asked.

'Princess Liz?', said the children. 'Who is she?'

'A queen who ruled over the land of Aurella. Her heart was pure, and she had a noble soul.'

The children began asking for more details about the princess.

Grandpa sat on a bench in the park and all the children gathered around him.

He began narrating his tale.

"In the days of yore, a kingdom called Aurella existed. A brave and kind-hearted princess ruled over the kingdom. It was a very prosperous kingdom until one day when the rains stopped. There was not a single drop of rain. The citizens waited for months together for a few drops of rain. Soon, there was a drought in the kingdom due to a lack of water. Not a single crop could be seen in the fields of Aurella. They tried to ask the other kingdoms for help, but even they refused, fearing that their grain stocks might get over too. The Princess went to an old saint. He told her,

'Your Highness, it is rumored that in the depths of the Claremont Forest, help will be given to the one with a noble heart. But you must overcome all kinds of challenges and reach the top of Caledonian Hill.'

The Princess immediately set off on her journey to Claremont Forest. The journey was smooth and pleasant for a while. The princess did not face any difficulties. However, after a while, Liz noticed that none of the trees in the forest bore any fruit or edible food. She had just a couple of apples that she'd found before.

Along the journey, she heard a pitiful voice. She got down from her horse and began to search for the source of the voice. She soon discovered a little bunny. She went closer and examined it. She saw quite a deep cut in the bunny's skin. She guessed that it might be from the strike of an arrow or any sharp twig lying on the ground. The princess quickly plucked a few strings of grass and other herbs in the forest, crushed them in her hand, and applied the mixture gently to the rabbit's wound. After a few minutes, the wound began to heal, and the princess set off on her journey again.

She came across a river. There was just a rope-like bridge to cross the river. So, she got off her horse and began to walk on it carefully. But she felt someone behind her and turned around to find a little girl standing behind her. The little girl said,

'Ma'am, I came here to play with my friends. My mother dropped me back then but now she is on the other side of the bridge, and I need to cross it over. Will you please help me?'

Liz knew that the later she found help, the more damage would be caused to her kingdom. However, the girl seemed desperate and in need of help. So, Liz decided to help her cross the rope and then went across it herself. The moment she stepped on the bridge with the little girl in front of her, the bridge gave a jerk, and all of a sudden, it seemed short. Liz was surprised but she had no time to figure out the reason behind it. So, she held the girl's hand and they both crossed the bridge in a remarkably short period. She dropped the little girl in her house and was overwhelmed to see the joy on the girl's and her mother's faces. Her mom thanked Liz immensely and invited her to stay. However, Liz said that she needed to reach the top of Caledonian Hill as soon as possible. They bid farewell to Liz and she continued her journey.

As the saint had said, she reached the door of Caledonian Hill after a couple of hours' journey. It was a very steep hill. But Liz was determined and began to climb the hill slowly. After hours of panting and climbing the hill, she finally reached the top. However, there was no one around and Liz was a little disappointed at first sight. But she began exploring the hill and after some time, she found an old hut. Inside, there was an old man who looked pale and exhausted. Lis entered and said,

'Sir, is anything wrong?'

'I haven't had anything to eat for over a week, my dear. My frail legs don't support me to get to the bottom of the hill and back up again with food.', said the old man in a weary tone.

His condition looked very pitiable indeed. His yellow rags of clothing lay open at his throat, revealing a very withered and worn-out body. Liz didn't have any food except for the very last apple she'd plucked from the tree at the beginning of her journey.

She said to the old man,

'Sir, I have nothing but a single apple. Would that suffice?'

'I will be grateful even the smallest morsel of food, my dear.', said the old man, his voice shaking.

Liz took out the last apple and gave it to the old man. He ate it and Liz was overjoyed with the satisfaction on his face.

He said, 'Where are you headed to, my dear?'

'I'm in search of help from the ancient magic that is said to be in these hills, sir.'

'May your noble heart guide you to success, dear.', blessed the old man.

Liz explored the hill, and she came across a cave. She went inside and saw three bright lights shining at the entrance of the cave. Suddenly, there was a flash of light, and in front of Liz, stood a fairy.

'I'm your fairy godmother Liz. I have been guarding the ancient magic of the Caledonian hills for Years. Do you see the three lights shining there? They indicate that you have been successful in all the tests that I put you through.'

'Tests?', said Liz, perplexed.

'Yes, my dear. Remember, the little bunny, the girl, and the old man whom you helped on your journey? Those were tests of character. In the first case, you looked across the form of the creature and helped it, even though it was an animal. Next, the bridge shortened when you decided to help the girl, even though you knew it would delay your journey. Lastly, you didn't have anything but the single apple, but you gladly offered it to the old man.'

'But, how do you know about all of this?', asked Liz.

'That's because I was the one who took the form of the bunny, girl, and the man.', said her fairy godmother, smiling.

Liz remembered the words of the saint she had sought help from.

'Help will be given to the one with a noble heart.'

All these three incidents were tests of character and personality, to find out whether she was worthy of the ancient magic.

'Liz, you have passed all three tests, with flying colours. Come further.'

Liz followed the fairy and saw a gem inside. It was one of the most exquisite gems she had ever seen in her life, and she had seen quite a lot.

'This,' said the fairy, 'is the gem of Agnes, the ancient ruler of the world. Agnes wanted to make sure that the gem did not fall into the wrong hands. So, I've been protecting it ever since she left this world. Now, it belongs to you, Liz. Use it wisely, just like Agnes once did.'

Again, there was a flash of light, and the fairy godmother disappeared. Liz took the gem in her hands and made her way back from the cave. However, something rooted her to the spot and a moment later, she found herself in Aurella. She smiled to herself and wished,

'Oh, magical stone! Please make the rain god grace us with his showers.'

Immediately, it began to rain. The rain was such that all the ponds, lakes, and even the smallest of water bodies were filled with water to the brim. Aurella was flourishing once more. Liz never told anyone about the gem but always protected it and kept it a secret, waiting to hand it over to a noble soul, like Agnes and the fairy godmother once did.

"Help will always be given to the one with a noble heart"

Author's Profile:

Subasree LS (Grade X) is an aspiring biostatistician with a deep passion for blending science with creativity. Known for her exceptional academic achievements, she is dedicated to advancing her knowledge in the field of biostatistics while nurturing a wide array of personal interests. In her spare time, Subasree enjoys reading fictional books, where she finds solace and inspiration. A keen chess player, she thrives on the intellectual challenge and strategic thinking that the game demands.

In addition to her academic and intellectual pursuits, Subasree is a gifted orator, captivating audiences with her eloquence and clarity of expression. Her talents extend to the arts as well, where she shines as a singer and artist, demonstrating a unique balance between analytical precision and creative flair. With her drive and diverse skill set, Subasree is on a promising path to make significant contributions both in her academic career and the broader world around her.

10

SCARY NIGHT

– ADVIKA YASHVI A C

It was 10 PM. I was alone at home when suddenly; I heard a knock on the door. I expected no one at the time, as all my family members had gone to attend a close family wedding. However, I was supposed to stay at home and study for my exam.

The repeated knocking at the door scared me to death. A chill went down my spine. Suddenly, the lights went off, and this only worsened my fear. Then I saw some shadows outside the window. My heartbeat increased as it was densely dark outside, and I couldn't imagine, even in my wildest thoughts, who could be there. I gathered up some courage, reached the window, slowly pulled the curtains, and looked outside. But the shadow was not clear at all, and it was not a single shadow but four or five shadows. This was enough for me to believe that some strangers were there at the door. I looked for my cricket bat, held it tightly, and reached the main door of the living room. Although it was a cold winter, I was still covered in sweat. With a sudden jerk, I opened the door and lifted my bat to hit, but I was surprised to see that they were my family members who had come early because I was alone at home. I felt relieved and embraced my mother tightly. That night, I slept with my mother. It was a scary night.

MORAL: The moral of the story is that fear can often cloud judgment. It's important to stay calm and think rationally, even in stressful situations.

Author's Profile:

Advika Yashvi, a Grade 3 student, is an attentive and focused young storyteller with a passion for English. She strives for perfection in everything she does, crafting heartfelt stories inspired by her life experiences. With her creativity and determination, Advika aims to become a renowned author in the future.

11

FAMILY POLITICS

– SAI SANKARI K

Hi, I'm the daughter of the millers, said Sophie. Suddenly, her brother Jack ran into her. He was running away from their mother, Mary; Jack was fidgeting with Mary's makeup. Sophie told me to take it, said Jack. Of Course, Mary had nothing to do with that. She was so surprised as Jack blamed her. She was fuming with anger. Her mother Mary believed him too, she was scolded terribly by her mother.

The next day, Sophie wanted revenge on her brother, so she was planning. However, her brother Jack was also planning to prank Sophie. Sophie decided she would tell her mother that he tore his report card before showing it to his mother, at that time Jack made a fake version of Sofie's report card and gave it to her mother; their plan backfired on both of them. Eventually, their Mother Mary found out what both of them were doing, Mary told them to apologize to each other, but they were so angry at their mother.

A few hours later, their dad, David, came home from work. Sophie and Jack both wanted to get revenge on their mother, so they planned to complain to David about Mary, claiming that she wasn't being kind. However, their plan backfired even more than they expected. Mary had already told David about what they did.

So, no matter how much they fought with each other they are still family and rest each and every one.

Author's Profile

Sai Sankari, an 11-year-old Grade 6 student, is broadminded and curious. She embraces challenges with enthusiasm and creativity. Her open-minded approach to learning makes her a promising young writer.

SUBASREE L S

SANA M

SAI AARUSH A

I AM AN AUTHOR

DUSHYANTH S

SAI SHARVAN M

M S DHONI
GLOBAL SCHOOL

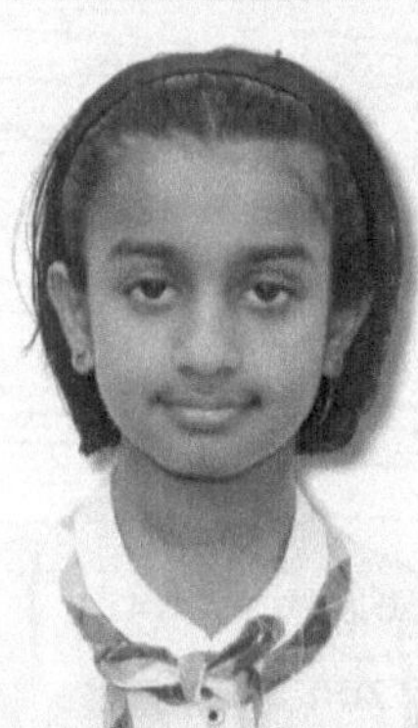

KRUTIKA R

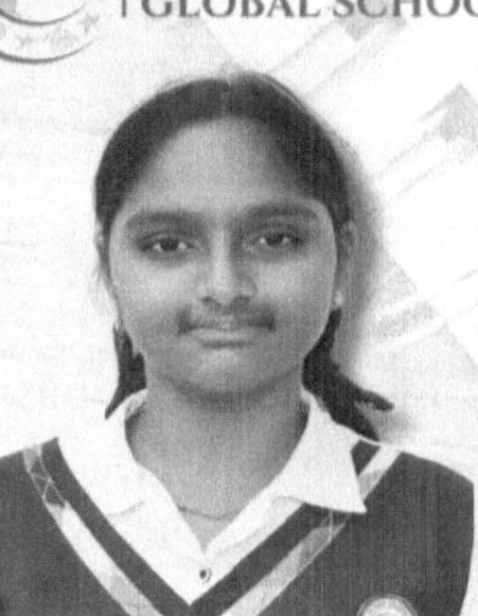

SAI RISHITHA T

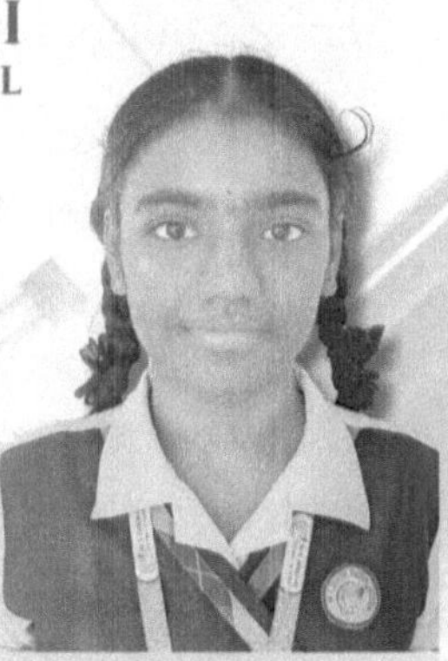

SUBASREE L S

MOWLINI B

SAI SANKARI K

ADVIKA YASHVI A C

12

BREAKING FREE FROM SELF-DOUBT

– RIDHANYA S

Once, in a bustling city, there lived a young woman named Maya. She had big dreams but was often weighed down by self-doubt. Her goal was to start a business, but every time she took a step forward, the fear of failure held her back. She watched others succeed and felt that she did not have what it took.

One day, Maya took a long walk in a nearby park and noticed a butterfly struggling to break free from its cocoon. She watched for hours, mesmerized by its persistence. Despite its tiny wings and fragile body, it pushed and stretched until, at last, it emerged. With newfound freedom, it took flight, soaring above the flowers with grace and strength. That sight sparked something in Maya. She realized that her struggles were like the butterfly's cocoon—a necessary part of her growth.

She decided to embrace her journey, no matter how difficult. Over time, she faced failures, but each one taught her valuable lessons. Slowly but surely, Maya built her business, and it became a success. Looking back, she understood that, like the butterfly, she needed those struggles to grow stronger. She now encourages others, sharing her story to inspire them to break free and fly.

MORAL: Embrace challenges; they make you stronger.

Author's Profile:

Ridhanya (Grade IV) is a responsible and talented student from grade IV who excels both in academics and extracurricular activities. Though she is shy, she possesses a quiet confidence that allows her to shine in her own way. Her dedication to everything she does promises a bright future ahead.

13

THE SIREN'S SONG

– PRANEETHA THANGARAJ

The sun began its descent, casting long shadows across the calm waters of the Caribbean Sea. A lone sailboat drifted slowly toward an unknown island, its shores glowing with a strange, almost supernatural light. Adrian, the sailor aboard the boat, felt an irresistible pull toward the island, his gaze fixed on the shore where an enchanting maiden stood, bathed in the soft glow of the fading sun. His eyes, once sharp, became clouded and distant, caught in the hypnotic beauty of the figure.

As the boat approached, the figure became clearer: a woman of breathtaking beauty, her emerald eyes gleaming like jewels, and her long black hair flowing like silk behind her pitch-black dress. Her sweet, melodic voice drifted across the water, a haunting melody that wrapped around Adrian's heart, urging him to come closer.

"Come with me," she called her voice like honey, laced with an allure that made his heart race. For a moment, he hesitated, doubts flitting through his mind. But her gaze, deep and loving, swept away any suspicion. The pull was too strong. Adrian steered his boat toward the shore, captivated by her presence.

Once ashore, the siren reached out and took his hand, her skin cool and smooth, leading him into a lush, enchanted forest. The trees towered above them, their leaves shimmering in the fading sunlight, whispering secrets only the wind could understand. The air was thick with the sweet scent of exotic flowers, and Adrian felt a thrill of excitement, believing he had stumbled upon a paradise untouched by time.

For hours, they wandered through the forest, talking and laughing as if they had known each other forever. The maiden—whose name, she told him, was Medusa—spoke of dreams and desires, of a world beyond the sea. But Adrian couldn't shake a growing sense of unease. When he took out his mirror compass to check his belongings, he noticed something odd: the beautiful woman did not cast a reflection. She seemed to disappear into the glass, a void where her image should have been.

Later, he saw her drinking a red substance from a vial—something that resembled blood. "It is animal blood," she explained with a smile that seemed almost too perfect. "Very good for health." Her voice was warm, but there was a coldness in her eyes that made Adrian's stomach twist with unease.

As they ventured deeper into the forest, the mood shifted. The trees grew twisted, their branches clawing at the sky like skeletal fingers. The sweet fragrance of flowers turned sour, replaced by a cold, graveyard-like smell that sent chills down Adrian's spine. Medusa's laughter, once soft and feminine, now carried a darker, more sinister edge. The path ahead seemed to disappear into an unnatural fog, and Adrian's heart began to race as he realized something was terribly wrong.

The atmosphere thickened with an overwhelming sense of dread. In a moment of clarity, Adrian understood. The beautiful maiden was not what she seemed. She was a siren, yes—but a rare and deadly kind: a vampire siren, one who lured sailors to their doom and drank their blood to enhance her beauty. His heart began to race once more—not with love, but with terror.

In a flash, her true form was revealed: a hideous monster with glowing red eyes and razor-sharp fangs, ready to pierce her prey. Her once-perfect beauty transformed into an eerie, fragile, bony face. She lunged at him with terrifying speed, her claws outstretched to claim him as her next victim.

Instinct kicked in. Adrian sprinted through the fog, desperation surging through his veins. The siren's laugh echoed in the distance, sending chills down his spine. The twisted trees seemed to close around him, their branches reaching for him like grasping hands. His heart pounded in his chest as he dashed toward the beach.

With every ounce of strength, he pushed forward, finally reaching the sailboat. He climbed aboard, his hands trembling as he untied the ropes. As the boat drifted away from the cursed island, Adrian looked back, his breath ragged. The haunting melody of the siren's song still echoed in his mind—a terrifying reminder of the beauty that concealed a deadly truth.

Author's Profile:

Praneetha, a grade VII student. is a passionate football enthusiast, known for her exceptional skills on the field. Whether it's dribbling past opponents or leading her team to victory, her love for the game drives her to constantly improve. Beyond sports, Praneetha possesses a vivid imagination, often coming up with creative solutions and new ideas that inspire those around her.

14

RACE FOR THE HIDDEN WEALTH

– SHRI RAM B L

It was the 2nd of March 2023 when Inspector James had been waiting for the arrival of subordinate Rocky who had gone to spy on the secret lair of the "Wanted Walter" a most wanted culprit. As he expected, he came with the next plan of Walter and his gang. They were to steal an ancient stone from the 'National Museum of California' as it had some old writings on it.

As soon as James received this information, he spoke with the museum management and replaced it with its duplicate. But the old writings on the stone seemed to confuse James and Rocky. It read as 'Give the key to the Joker in the wild.' They thought that surely Walter must have the key. But what does the phrase "Joker in the wild' mean? Rocky was again given the mission of venturing into Walter's lair and looting the key from him. Meanwhile, James was involved in the research of finding the meaning of the phrase.

Rocky ensured that nobody was in the lair. He then entered and stole the key from a shelf. When Walter returned and saw that the key was missing, he immediately checked the stone. It was written as "Your plan will never succeed!'. He suspected it to be James as he was the only police officer who was a threat to Walter. He immediately ordered a group of his men to follow James from that point of time and to intimate him with everything.

When Rocky returned, he found that James solved the phrase. He found out that the one and only Zoo which had a circus in it was opened in Sao Paulo in 1968. He believed that the chief joker of that circus might know something about the mystery. When James showed the key to the joker and inquired about the phrase, the joker handed over to him an ancient box saying, 'This box has been given to my great grandfather by a man who told me that this box contains information about the treasure should be given only to the person who brings both the stone and the key. It has been passed down for generations, and now that by handing over this box to you, I feel relieved to complete this task.

Author's Profile:

Shriram B L (Grade VIII) an adventurous storyteller, is the author of Race for the Hidden Wealth. His story is an exciting journey filled with suspense, mystery, and the thrill of treasure hunting. Sriram's writing draws readers into a world of daring exploration and high-stakes quests, showcasing his flair for adventure and imaginative plot twists. His narrative captures the spirit of discovery, making for a truly engaging read.

15

THE RAIN THAT NEVER FALLS

– LARVIKA P

In the small town of Esperanza, the sky was always grey, and it hadn't rained in years. The townspeople remembered a legend about a rainmaker who could summon storms; everyone thought he had some superpower in his hand, but sadly he had vanished long ago. Rebecca, a curious girl with curly hair who was in her first year in high school, loved to explore the meadows. One day, she came across an old oak tree with a silver bell at its roots.

As it looked suspicious, she went near to look at it. It was an ancient silver bell, just half the size of a finger! She tried pulling it from the root, but it was hard, so she got help from her friends, who applied all their energy together to pull it out. With a jingling sound, they took it out. When she shook it, a soft sound filled the air, which was so pleasant to hear. Suddenly, dark clouds began to swirl above her, and rain started to fall—beautiful, sparkling drops that danced on the ground.

Excited, Rebecca twirled in the rain as the townsfolk rushed outside, amazed by the sight. The rain brought life back to their dry town, filling it with joy and colors. The people sang together, and children danced in the rain, their voices mixing with the falling rain. From that day on, Esperanza was transformed into a beautiful town with colorful flowers and joyful people. Rebecca became a local heroine, visiting the oak tree often to hear its magical stories. Though it never rained the same way again, the magic of that day reminded everyone that hope, and belief could bring life back to their world.

Author's Profile:

Larvika, a vibrant student of grade IX, brings imagination and energy into everything she does. With a love for dancing, drawing, and reading fantasy stories, she is especially inspired by tales like "*The 5 on a Treasure Island by Enid Blyton*". Her latest fantasy story reflects her creativity and fascination with magical worlds. Larvika's love for the rainy season adds a poetic touch to her work, and her unique perspective shines in each story she creates.

16

THE GATEWAY

– VEDANTH K

In the year 2145, humanity was on the verge of a new era. After decades of intense research and engineering, Dr. Locke finally revealed "The Gateway," his most ambitious invention. Made of a rare material called Nebulite, the device gleamed under the facility's lights, capable of bending space and time to allow instant travel across galaxies.

At the Helios Research Facility, Locke prepared to activate The Gateway, feeling a strange unease. Scientists, government officials, and reporters gathered to witness history in the making. Millions around the world were tuned in, awaiting the start of what could be a revolutionary age. But as the final moments ticked by, one question hung in Locke's mind: Could something this powerful really be controlled?

Locke took a deep breath and flicked the switch. The machine rumbled to life, and a bright blue portal formed, swirling with alien colours that seemed to shift and shimmer. The crowd gasped as the portal stabilized, offering a glimpse into a distant world.

To mark the moment, Locke stepped into the portal. On the other side, he found himself on an alien landscape where bioluminescent plants cast an eerie glow under the light of three moons. Strange symbols etched into rocks pulsed with a mysterious energy. But suddenly, a loud alarm blared from the facility—the portal was becoming unstable. Locke hurried back, barely making it through before the gateway closed.

Back at the facility, applause broke out, but Locke stood in silence, haunted by what he had seen. The Gateway was indeed a marvel of science, yet it was also a reminder of the unknown dangers that lay ahead. As he looked out at the cheering crowd, he couldn't shake the thought: "What have I unleashed?"

Author's Profile:

Vedanth, a 13-year-old Grade 8 student, is a passionate science fiction writer with a vivid imagination. His stories explore futuristic technologies and the ethical dilemmas they bring, blending creativity with a love for science. In The Gateway, Vedanth delves into humanity's ambitions and the mysteries of the universe. His optimistic nature fuels his belief in balancing curiosity with caution. Outside writing, he enjoys exploring scientific concepts and dreaming of humanity's cosmic future.

17

THE SHINBI'S APARTMENT

– K S KAVINILA

A family consisting of a mother, father, older sister, and younger sister lived in an apartment known as Shinbi's Apartment. The fact that a goblin named Shinbi lived inside a well was only known to the sisters. The Webbed Spider was a ghost that existed once. The sisters possessed a button that, when used, could call forth any ghost—but only once. Therefore, they called upon Shinbi as a solution. They could see how the ghost died since they had a ghost ball.

One day, a mother purchased a spider for her son. Her son was playing with the spider when, suddenly, the spider emerged from its box and made its way toward the balcony. The young boy rushed to capture it and nearly fell off the balcony. The mother, who witnessed this, immediately left her job and hurried to save her child. She managed to rescue her child, but she and the spider fell from the balcony. The ghost was dubbed the Webbed Spider because her spirit merged with the spider.

Since the ghost was in the form of a spider, the sisters and Shinbi used magical origami papers to make a bird, but they were unable to fight it. Then, the Webbed Spider's child suddenly appeared and ordered her to stop. She listened to him and left for Heaven because it was her child. The Webbed Spider's ghost ball, which allows the sisters to call forth any ghost they like, was given to them.

Author's Profile:

K S Kavinila, of grade IV is the emerging writer who touches the aspects of this generation. Apart from writing stories, she is a dedicated dance artist, who loves reading stories. She is an ingenious person with appreciable qualities in her.

18

THE MAGIC BRACELET

– ASHMITHA SRI S

One sunny afternoon, 12-year-old Tara stumbled upon a peculiar bracelet lying half-buried in the dirt on her way home from school. It looked old, almost ancient, with a delicate band of metal wrapped around stones that glimmered in the sunlight. Intricate symbols, once she couldn't quite recognize, were carved around each of the colorful stones. Intrigued, Tara picked it up, brushed off the dirt, and carefully slipped it onto her wrist.

The moment she wore the bracelet, her surroundings blurred, and suddenly, Tara found herself standing on a beach with towering waves crashing at her feet. The ocean was wild, and the wind roared around her. She gasped, realizing that just moments ago she'd been on a quiet street. Frightened, she quickly took the bracelet off, and in an instant, she was back on her usual path home, with the sound of cars and the familiar row of houses around her. Shaken but curious, she decided to keep the bracelet, tucking it safely into her pocket.

The next day, the mystery of the bracelet nagged at her. During her lunch break, she couldn't resist putting it on again. This time, she was transported to the snow-capped peaks of a mountain. Cold air whipped her face, and she could see endless miles of white snow and rocky cliffs stretching beneath a deep blue sky. She quickly took off the bracelet, her heart racing as she returned to the schoolyard, hidden behind a tree.

Soon, putting on the bracelet became a daily ritual. Each time, Tara was taken to a new place—the bustling streets of an old city, the quiet serenity of a misty forest, even a golden desert under the glow of a setting sun. It was like a passport to hidden worlds. Her little secret became the best part of her day, and she began reading up on the places she "visited," making notes and comparing them with pictures she found online.

But one evening, she decided to wear the bracelet right before bed. This time, instead of beautiful scenes, she found herself in a dark, damp cave. Shadows moved along the walls, and eerie red eyes gleamed from the darkness, watching her. Her heart pounded, and as she tried to move, she felt frozen, as if her legs were glued to the ground. The red eyes grew larger, closer. With a scream, she yanked off the bracelet, finding herself safely back in her bedroom, her heart racing and her palms sweaty.

The bracelet lay there on her bed, silent and harmless. But now, Tara was unsure. Was this mysterious bracelet truly a gift, or was it a curse leading her to dangerous places? She wanted to keep exploring, yet the memory of those glowing red eyes haunted her thoughts.

Over the next few days, she thought about the bracelet's magic and the unknown risks it held. Maybe, she realized, some mysteries were better left unsolved. She put the bracelet away in a small box, uncertain if she would ever wear it again, but knowing she had experienced something truly magical and unforgettable.

MORAL: Curiosity can lead to wondrous adventures, but wisdom means recognizing the limits of what we explore.

Author's Profile:

Ashmitha Sri, an 11-year-old in Grade 6, is a quiet individual who speaks through her actions and writing. Her introspective nature allows her to express deep thoughts without words. She is known for her thoughtfulness and creativity.

19

REVITALISATION

– ASMITHA A

On a fine day, Izzy's father was reading the newspaper when he got excited and quickly turned on the TV. He hadn't seen Izzy in ages and missed her but always encouraged her to follow her passion and talent. He still remembered the day she left for university, assuring her of his support and quoting William Ward, "Curiosity is the wick in the candle of learning. Go make me proud, dear." As these memories surfaced and his wife joined him, a show began on the TV.

The title displayed: "Revitalization of Culture Starting from Never Isle – A Journey Led True."

The interviewer welcomed Izzy and her team, eager to learn about their latest adventure. Izzy's eyes sparkled with excitement as she began, "Honestly, it's the mystery of the place. Never Isle is one of those rare places mostly spoken of in folklore—a barren land that somehow came to life. The more we discovered, the more questions arose. We just had to see it for ourselves."

The interviewer leaned in, intrigued. "And you've uncovered some fascinating stories about the island's origins, I hear?"

Jake, the team's archaeologist and an excellent researcher when it comes to physical artifacts, took a deep breath before answering. "Yes, absolutely. The island's history sounds mythical. Apparently, volcanic activity—like what formed the Andaman and Nicobar Islands—created Never Isle. And while Greenland may be the largest island today, Never Isle has a unique twist: it has twice Greenland's population! Most of the people here are Tamil, which initially surprised us."

"Twice the population of Greenland?" the interviewer echoed in amazement. "That's incredible! How did the Tamil connection come about?"

Jake explained, "Locals believe their ancestors traveled from India thousands of years ago. They tell of a princess named Matria, blessed by Mother Earth herself. When she set foot on the island, the barren land blossomed with life. She is known as *Bhoomi Natamaiyar*, the 'Queen of Earth,' and holds a significant place in their identity. Temples dedicated to her are scattered across the island, with inscriptions in ancient Tamil resembling Pallava and early Chola scripts. It's a mystery, as there are no records of British or Portuguese contact, yet these temples have remained untouched."

Fascinated, the interviewer asked, "So Matria is seen as a divine figure in their culture?"

"Definitely," Padmanaban replied. "Her story is woven into every part of life here. But it's more than just a legend; it's the foundation of their identity and heritage. There's a deep respect for nature in everything they do."

"What other aspects of Never Isle's culture have you noticed?" asked the interviewer, sensing there was much more to uncover.

Izzy chimed in, "The sense of community and unity here is incredible. This island is a close-knit place where tradition connects everyone. Their respect for nature is profound, not just because of Matria's story but also due to centuries-old customs of coexistence. The environment here is pristine—almost no pollution. It feels like a sanctuary."

The interviewer smiled, captivated. "It sounds like a place out of time. How are the younger generations handling such a unique heritage?"

"They're not only proud of it but also incredibly forward-thinking," Izzy said. "The youth here are dedicated to preserving the island's legacy, yet they have this energy and drive to bring in fresh ideas. They're passionate about balancing tradition with modern ideals and are approaching it carefully."

The interviewer nodded thoughtfully. "It's amazing how the past and future coexist here. Are there any mysteries still left unsolved?"

Jake exclaimed, "Absolutely. We met a historian who took on the same challenge as we did. He said that we've only scratched the surface. Imagine—only about 20% of our oceans are fully explored. Who knows what secrets lie beneath? Never Isle still holds countless stories waiting to be uncovered. Its legends, its ancient writings—each discovery only deepens the mystery."

"What's next for you and the team?" the interviewer asked, sensing the adventure wasn't over.

Izzy glanced at her team, smiling. "For now, we're taking it all in. This trip has shown us how much there is to learn and protect. We're documenting everything, from historical insights to ecological observations, so we can share the story of Never Isle with the world."

"Thank you, Izzy, and team," the interviewer said warmly. "It's been wonderful hearing about this journey. We can't wait to read more about Never Isle and its remarkable story."

As the audience applauded, the doorbell rang. Izzy's mother answered it, and there stood none other than Izzy, home to surprise her parents. Her father, proud and beaming, embraced her warmly, enjoying every moment of their reunion.

The story of Never Isle takes us into a whirlwind of mysteries, culture, and modernization. The people honour the spirit of Mother Earth in a beautiful way. Still, many cultures around the world remain unheard of, whether due to challenges or chosen isolation. Young people like Izzy and her team are needed to preserve cultures, languages, and people across the globe.

Author's Profile:

Asmitha (Grade IX) is a talented and imaginative student known for her artistic flair and friendly nature. Her love for drawing and creativity shines through in her storytelling, which often transports readers to magical realms of fantasy and adventure. With aspirations of becoming an IAS officer, Asmitha combines her ambition with a vivid imagination that captivates and inspires. Her latest story is a thrilling adventure filled with wonder, and it reflects her unique ability to bring the extraordinary to life. We are excited to see where her journey as a storyteller will lead!

20

THE ENIGMAS MAGIC OF NATURE

– DHIVYESH JEYAMURUGAN

Once upon a time, when the Weather Man was going down a dusty country lane, he fell over a stone. He was carrying a rain spell in a little pot and some of it spilt when he fell.

"Bother!" said the Weatherman, sitting up and rubbing his knees. "I've spoiled my spell. Now we shall have too little rain!"

"You spilled it on me, you spilled it on me!" cried a tiny voice crossly. "It hurts! It smarts! I don't like it. Take it away!"

"Oh dear!" said the Weatherman in alarm and looked to see if the spell had fallen on a pixie or elf. But it hadn't. It had fallen on a small plant with scarlet flowers, tiny and star-like. It was the scarlet pimpernel.

"I'm so sorry," said the Weatherman and got out his handkerchief. He wiped the little plant, but it still made a great fuss.

"It's horrid! It stings! The rain spell is much too strong, I don't like it."

"Shut up your little red flowers then," said the Weatherman. "It won't sting so much if you do. I'm really very sorry, Pimpernel."

He picked up his jar. It was only half full now. Dear, dear, what a lot must have been spilled over the poor little pimpernel! No wonder it had stung.

"I shall be dreadfully afraid of the rain now," said the pimpernel. "I want an umbrella in case the rain comes. That horrid rain spell has made me frightened of a rainstorm."

"Oh, don't be silly," said the Weatherman. "Whoever heard of a plant wanting an umbrella? Of course, I shan't get you one. Be sensible."

He went on his way and left the little pimpernel staring closely at the big golden sun above. "I shall always close my petals now when I know that rain is coming," it said to itself. "Always. If I don't, that rain spell may set to work again when it rains and be stingy and smart."

The next morning, when the sky was as blue as forget-me-nots, the pimpernel suddenly shut up all its scarlet flowers. They closed very tightly indeed. Pip and Twinkle, two pixies passing by, called to it in surprise.

"What's the matter? Why are you shutting? Is it your early closing day, Pimpernel?"

"Don't be stupid," said the pimpernel, opening one small scarlet eye. "I don't have early closing days. I'm shutting my flowers because I know it's going to rain. I've had a rain spell spilled on me. That's how I know."

"Storyteller! Don't tell lies!" said Pip. "There isn't a cloud in the sky."

"Well, you take my advice and go home for your umbrellas," said the pimpernel. But the pixies laughed and went on their way. Will you believe it, in an hour the sky clouded over and big drops of rainfall, soaked Pip and Twinkle to the skin! How they wished they had taken the pimpernel's advice. They went to talk to it again the next day.

"Pimpernel! You are very clever. Will you come and live in the garden beside our little house, so that you can always tell us what the weather is going to be? Then we shall never get soaked again."

"Yes. I'll come. Dig me up carefully, roots and all," said the pimpernel, feeling rather proud to be asked to grow in a garden, for it was really only a wildflower, a tiny weed.

So, Pip and Twinkle dug it up very carefully, took it home in their little wheelbarrow, and planted it in their garden. They watered it, made a fuss of it, and then went to get their tea.

"We must hurry because we have to go to a meeting at six," said Pip. Before they went, they ran over to the Pimpernel. Dear me, what was this? It was shutting up all its petals, though the sun was shining brightly.

"It's going to rain," it told the pixies. "It is. I can feel it coming. I shall always know when the rain is about now!" The pimpernel spoke the truth. It does

Always know when it's going to rain. Would you like to prove it? Very well, then, dig up a little plant, put it into a flowerpot, and keep it on your windowsill. It will tell you truly whenever it is going to rain, so you will always know when to take an umbrella or not. Strange, isn't it?

Author's Profile:

Dhivyesh Jeyamurugan (Grade X) is an aspiring data analyst with a strong passion for both analytical thinking and creative expression. With a keen interest in historical novels, he enjoys immersing himself in stories that explore the past and offer deep insights into human nature and society. When he's not reading, Dhivyesh spends his time drawing, channelising his creativity through art, and playing badminton, which helps him stay active and focused.

Driven by a curiosity for data and patterns, Dhivyesh is determined to pursue a career as a data analyst, where he aims to make meaningful contributions through his sharp analytical skills. His diverse interests reflect his well-rounded personality, blending his love for history, art, and sports with his academic ambitions.

21

THE GOLDEN COIN

– NIDHARSWA P

Once upon a time, there was a boy named Rohan. He was nine years old and in Grade V. Rohan was a little naughty, and every day, he walked to school. One morning, as he walked along the street, he found a shining gold coin that sparkled like the sun. Curiously, Rohan picked it up and took it with him to school.

As he continued walking, something magical happened. The gold coin suddenly transported him into the future. Rohan was amazed as he saw the world around him—houses shaped like diamonds that towered high into the sky. He wandered through this futuristic world until he found a house that looked familiar.

Thinking it was his home, he knocked on the door, hoping to find his parents. But to his surprise, a man and his pet answered instead. His parents were nowhere to be found. It was getting late, and Rohan felt tired. He looked for a place to sleep and eventually found a quiet spot under a tree. As he fell into a deep sleep, he was filled with awe and confusion about the strange world he was in.

The next morning, Rohan woke up and discovered he was back in his own time, standing on the same street where he had found the gold coin. He noticed a drainage ditch nearby and, feeling relieved to be home, threw the coin into it. As he ran back to his house, everything seemed normal again.

Rohan realized that what he had experienced was just a wonderful dream, but it was a dream he would never forget.

Author's Profile:

Nidharswa of grade V is a creative and imaginative Grade V student with a strong interest in academics. He is a positive and enthusiastic student who actively participates in class activities. With a growing attention to detail and an openness to refine his work, he is a quick learner and a disciplined child.

22

THE MAGIC RUG

– DIYA NIRANJAN

Once upon a time, in a beautiful village, there was a little cottage. A family of four lived in that little cottage: a father, a mother, a sister named Lilly, and a little brother named John. One day, they bought a rug, not knowing it was truly a special type of rug.

That night, John and Lilly shared the rug. When they were about to sleep, the rug started to talk. "Hello, I am Tom, and I am a special type of rug. I can talk, and I can take you on an adventure if you both wish."

John and Lilly replied, "Yes, of course! We love adventures, Tom!" Then, John and Lilly flew from the bedroom through the window, like birds, into the sky.

They saw clouds shaped like fish, trees, and unicorns. As they flew through the sky, they noticed a reddish-golden light. They were curious to see what the bright golden light was. As they flew closer, they were amazed to see that it was the city of unicorns. They saw plenty of unicorns racing across the city.

They met a unicorn named Jasmine and became friends with her. Jasmine told them all about Unicorn City. Tom, John, and Lilly gratefully thanked Jasmine for sharing everything about the city. Moreover, John and Lilly wholeheartedly thanked Tom for taking them on such an astonishing adventure.

They returned home and decided to share this amazing adventure with their parents. Their parents were also amazed to hear what their kids had told them. They all lived happily ever after, cherishing the memories.

Author's Profile:

Diya (Grade IV) has a bright and positive personality. She approaches each day with a smile, spreading joy to everyone around her. She lifts the spirits of those around her, even during challenging times. Diya is known for her exemplary manners and respectful nature, both towards her peers and teachers which eventually makes her a role model for her classmates and community.

S RIDHANYA

VEDANTH K

ASMITHA

PRANEETHA
THANGARAJ

DHIVYESH
JEYAMURUGAN

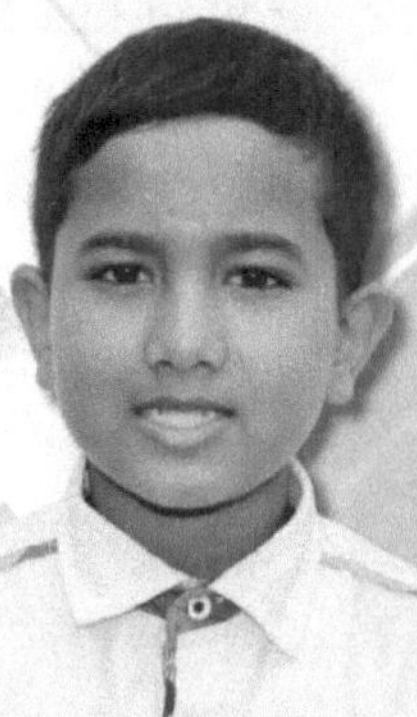

SHRIRAM B L

KAVINILA S K

NIDHARSWA P

LARVIKA P

ASHMITHA SRI S

DIYA NIRANJAN

23

KINDNESS IS ALWAYS GOOD

– CHARULEKHA S

In a small town called Monique, there lived a kind boy named Ravi. He lived in an orphanage and was special because he always helped others, becoming a beacon of kindness. Unlike many people in his town, who were often mean and sad, Ravi was warm and caring. He showed everyone how nice it is to be kind. Sadly, most people didn't realize how important it was to be friendly and share happiness.

One fateful day, a monster appeared in the center of Monique. Towering and ferocious, he was a remarkable sight, instantly drawing the gaze of every townsfolk. As his massive form loomed over the landscape, panic spread. The streets seemed to shrink beneath his weight, and the terrifying roar that erupted from his mouth sent shivers down the spines of all who looked his way. It felt as though half the town had been swallowed by this monstrous creature, leaving the residents trembling in fear, unsure of what would happen next.

The huge monster roared, "I will eat one of you or the whole town! You have one hour to decide who will be eaten by me."

During that tense hour, no one stepped forward to volunteer. Each person insisted, "You go! I won't go!" Their selfishness and fear were evident as the clock ticked down. Then, without warning, the monster appeared, and all their arguments ceased, leaving them frozen in terror at what lay before them.

The monster looked down at the crowd and asked, "Who wants to be eaten by me?"

Fear swept through the group as his question hung in the air. Everyone began to shout and argue among themselves, trying to avoid the monster's stare. Some said the bravest person should step forward, while others argued that no one should volunteer. With a deafening roar, the monster bellowed, "I'll devour this entire town if no one steps forward!"

At that moment, Ravi confidently stepped forward, his voice steady. "I will willingly become your feast!"

The fearsome monster began to shimmer and shift, its jagged edges softening and its menacing form dissolving into radiant light. As the glow enveloped it, the creature transformed into the divine figure of Lord Krishna. Everyone was filled with a mix of surprise and shock.

Lord Krishna turned to Ravi with a compassionate expression and gently asked, "Ravi, what inspired you to put yourself in harm's way for the sake of others?"

Ravi replied, "Had I not volunteered to confront the monster, the entire town would have faced destruction. Such an outcome would truly have been unfortunate."

Lord Krishna was moved by Ravi's heartfelt response and generously granted him a beautiful boon. "From this moment on, Ravi will be able to live peacefully with his parents for as long as he desires."

Brimming with gratitude, Ravi conveyed his heartfelt thanks to Lord Krishna, who then gently faded away, leaving a lasting sense of hope and inspiration.

From that day forward, the town embraced its new name, "The Kind City." It was heartwarming to see how everyone began to share kindness, creating a sense of community and warmth.

MORAL: Choosing to be kind can lead to remarkable outcomes.

Author's Profile:

Charulekha of grade V is a responsible and active student in class, consistently demonstrating a strong commitment to her work. Her deep knowledge and excellent observation skills are truly remarkable, allowing her to grasp complex concepts with ease. Kind-hearted and highly intellectual, Charulekha approaches every task with smart strategies and a thoughtful mindset. She is dedicated to doing her best and is always willing to help others with a positive attitude. A true classroom asset, Charulekha sets an inspiring example for her peers.

24

THE JOURNEY IN TIME

– VIDHYUTH SHADAMARSHAN A

Introduction

Have you ever imagined traveling through time? Picture yourself on a train journey that suddenly lands you in the distant past—a world without any of the modern things we know today.

Now, let me take you on a journey through time with the story of Jack and Hamza.

The Train

It was a bright, sunny morning, and Jack was playing soccer in the park with his friend Hamza. Jack loved soccer, especially with Hamza. They were opposites—Hamza was tall, thin, and fair-skinned, while Jack was shorter, plump, and dark-haired. Their summer holidays had just begun, and they were thrilled.

Jack was heading to his grandmother's house that day. At around nine in the morning, he left the house, carrying a backpack and a small statue as a gift for his grandparents. After a long ride through city traffic, they reached the train station at ten.

As he boarded the train, Jack suddenly felt an eerie sense of dread, but he decided to ignore it. Not long after, he heard a chilling voice in his head say, "Well done, Jack. You have almost predicted the future." He shrugged it off as his imagination.

At the second stop, a hooded man wearing a dark jacket boarded the train. His hood was so thick it was impossible to see his face. Sitting down, the man reached into his bag, pulled out a small remote, and pressed a big red button. Then, he turned toward Jack, saying in the same icy voice, "Time to take you on a journey into the past. Buckle up!" A thick fog began to cloud Jack's mind, and the last thing he remembered was the sound of terrified screams all around him.

Meeting Dinosaurs: A New Discovery

When Jack awoke, he found himself in a dense forest. To his surprise, the first person he saw was Hamza—wearing the same jacket as the mysterious man on the train! "Hamza, was that you? How could you do this?" Jack demanded, sounding both confused and serious.

Hamza chuckled. "Relax, Jack! I just wanted to test out my new time machine. And you were the first person that came to mind! I knew you'd be on that train, so I got on at the second stop to surprise you."

"But what about the voice I heard?" Jack asked. At that moment, another figure stepped out from behind Hamza.

"That was my friend," Hamza explained, pointing to the person who'd helped him with his plan.

With everything explained, Hamza suggested they explore their surroundings. "Come on! Let's go see the T. rex that lives here!" he said excitedly. They began running through the forest, eager to find the famous dinosaur.

When they finally spotted the T. rex, it was towering and ancient-looking, like something from a dream. The creature turned its massive head, peered down at them, and let out a deafening roar. To their surprise, it bent down and winked at them! But then, the T. rex called for its friends, and soon, more dinosaurs emerged from the forest.

Jack and Hamza ran faster than they'd ever run before, catching glimpses of Archosaurs, Stegosaurs, and more along the way. As they sprinted, Hamza suddenly pointed at the sky, yelling, "Look, Jack! Is that an asteroid? The one that wiped out the dinosaurs? Run faster!"

Jack glanced up and saw a bright object streaking through the sky. "Hamza, is your remote working?" he shouted.

"Not yet! But maybe we can find shelter!" Hamza replied. Thinking quickly, Jack spotted a cave nearby and dashed toward it, with Hamza close behind.

The T. rex couldn't fit inside the cave, so it soon gave up and left. From the safety of the cave, they watched as sparks filled the sky and the ground shook. The dinosaurs had vanished, wiped out by the powerful blast.

After a while, Hamza's remote finally started working again. He pressed the button, and in an instant, Jack found himself at his grandmother's house. His mother was waiting there, worried. "Where have you been? I was so scared!" she exclaimed.

"Long story," he replied with a smile, then headed to his room, eager to write down every detail of his adventure.

MORAL: Animals, even the ancient ones, can teach us incredible lessons and make unforgettable friends on our journeys.

Author's Profile:

Vidhyuth from grade V is a highly responsible student with a strong sense of accountability at a young age. His natural talent shines through in a variety of subjects and activities. Whether it's academic achievements or leadership roles in group settings, Vidhyuth demonstrates an ability to excel and take initiative. His creativity allows him to stand out in both academics and extracurriculars.

25

SAMMY SNAIL

– RASHMI M

Once upon a time, there lived a small snail named Sammy Snail, who lived with his parents. Sammy also had a grandmother, but she was not feeling well. One day, Sammy's parents went to the market to buy vegetables and other necessities for the house. They left Sammy with his grandmother.

Since Sammy's grandmother was not feeling well, she could not play with Sammy. So, Sammy sat by the window near a table with a chair. Then, the phone rang—tring, tring. Sammy picked up the phone and said, "Hello! Who is this?" It was Wolfy Wolf, the kidnapper. He replied, "Hello! I am your father. What do you want as a gift?"

Sammy really thought it was his father and answered Wolfy's question by saying, "I want a toy car." Wolfy asked Sammy for his address and told him he would meet him at 3:00 PM. Sammy waited for a long time by the window, waiting for Wolfy to arrive.

Wolfy arrived after a long wait, but he had no gift with him. He sat down on the couch and began drinking a glass of water. After a few minutes, Wolfy tried to kidnap Sammy, but

Sammy shouted, "Help, help me!" Tiger, the police officer, who was passing by, heard Sammy's shout and rushed into the house. He quickly understood what had happened and arrested Wolfy. Wolfy was later sent to prison.

Afterward, Sammy and his family lived happily ever after.

MORAL: Don't talk to strangers or accept anything from them.

Author's Profile:

Rashmi M. is a grade VII student, born on November 12, 2012, in Neyveli. She is fond of playing with younger kids and has a calm personality. Her hobby is playing badminton, and her ambition is to become both an excellent player and a novelist.

26

YOU'LL BE BACK

– SAMYUKTHA BASKARAN

I suppose my story starts this way, as a kid I grew up in a rather rural area, but I was happy, I lived with my parents.

There were often places where we nearly failed to make ends meet, so you sacrificed a few things, adding to the fact that our financial condition wasn't very stable, to say the least. As a child who was taught that education was the only way to break away from the chains of poverty and experience success {happiness},

Being a data scientist seemed to be the key, and since there were better chances abroad, I decided to go to the US, my parents begged me not to go but I was determined

So here I am, it's

26th July 2004

And I've just moved to my shady apartment last week (yay) I believe I got this place from eBay (don't ask me how)

So far, it's just me, dusty floors and God knows what demons from Australia decided to rent here. Anyway, what do u expect from Alabama, I also have upstairs neighbors who seem to be Russian and have a fixation on partying at 3 am. (I asked if I could join, they said no)

Moving on I realized that I needed food which meant I needed a job, Luckily I got to be a cashier and Wendy's

Turns out half the people speak in Russian, why? Alabama, I guess

One time I tried saying "Have a good day" in Russian to a customer but blurted out "vykhodi za menya " which means "marry me" in Russian. The customer looked… well uhh… traumatized as she walked out.

The job pays barely so I can't make ends meet but this time … it's harder… I had my parents to cope with but now…

3rd August 2007

It's been 3 years…huh… here I am "successful" I have secured my job as a data scientist and even paid off my parent's debts. As I sit here, I can't help but think that the many years of blood, sweat, and tears I shed to sit here, all just gave me fake friends, unfaithful relations, pain, agony, and… money…just like they promised. but this isn't what I want. is it? but… why don't I feel the joy I once had previously, in this new life that gave me success, growth, money, fame, stability, identity

Why do I long for love, happiness, care, support, and my parents, all the things I once had?

Is this really what success and happiness is?

Is this the life I have been longing for?

How corrupted has humanity become to make me believe that… this life is what I need? When truly… all I needed were my real friends, my parents, and their adorning love for me

Mom and Dad, you were right, and so, … I'll be back.

Author's Profile:

Samyuktha Baskaran, a talented Grade 8 student, is the author of You'll Be Back. Through her reflective storytelling, she delves into themes of ambition, family, and the true meaning of success. Samyuktha's narrative captures the emotional journey of self-discovery, blending humor and sincerity to engage readers. Her writing showcases a deep understanding of personal values and the importance of staying connected to one's roots.

27

TIMEKEEPER'S BORROWED MINUTES

– HRIDHIK KANNAN VELAVAR

An ancient, dusty clock tower in a small town wasn't just any clock tower; it was home to the world's only Timekeeper, a slightly crazy, middle-aged man named Marlon. His job? Making sure every second ticked just as it should, without any hiccups. But Marlon had a little secret: he occasionally borrowed a few minutes here and there for "personal use."

One Tuesday morning, he felt particularly lazy and borrowed five minutes just to finish his morning breakfast. Later in the day, he borrowed another twenty for a nap. Soon enough, he was in the habit of pocketing minutes like candy, which he'd keep in a jar on his desk labeled "Emergency Time." The townsfolk didn't notice at first, but over time, things started to get… odd. School days felt like they were flying by while doctor appointments dragged on forever. Some people would swear they'd been in line at the bakery for hours, only to realize they had been served in five minutes.

One day, a little girl named Lucy, curious and nosy as ever, managed to sneak into the clock tower and catch Marlon red-handed, sneaking a few minutes to stretch his lunch break. She gasped, "You're stealing time!"

"Borrowing, my dear, borrowing! It's for perfectly good reasons!" Marlon said with a grin, trying to look innocent while clutching a handful of seconds. But Lucy wasn't convinced. "Give them back, or I'm telling everyone."

With a heavy sigh, Marlon reluctantly unscrewed the jar of "Emergency Time" and released all the minutes he'd borrowed over the years. Time in the town stumbled and returned to normal. People in the bakery line suddenly realized they hadn't been waiting that long, school days became impossibly slow again, and doctors' appointments were, well, back to being miserable.

As Lucy skipped down the clock tower stairs, Marlon muttered, "Well, there goes my afternoon nap." He made a silent promise to only borrow minutes in emergencies—or for really, really good meals!

Author's Profile:

Hridhik Kannan Velavar, a dedicated student from IX, is known for his passion for athletics, creativity in crafts, and love for gaming. As the assistant sports captain, he brings determination and leadership to his role, inspiring his peers both on and off the field. With a clear ambition to pursue Aerospace Engineering, Hridhik combines his love for science and exploration with a strong work ethic. His drive and focus promise an exciting future.

28

IN EVERY WOMEN

– SHANTHANA SHRI T

Once, there lived a joyful family known as the Sharma family. The family included Mr. Sharma, his wife, Mrs. Rakul Sharma, and their two daughters, Vinothitha and Nithya. They lived happily together. One day, the two girls went on a school-organized trip. Vinothitha was fair-skinned, while Nithya was dark-skinned, and some students often teased Nithya, not realizing how deeply it hurt her. Nithya, feeling very upset, wandered off alone and missed the school bus, which left her stranded on campus. She was heartbroken when she realized she had missed her ride home. Hidden from view, she couldn't be seen by the security guard who locked the gate.

Another complication was that she had already marked her attendance, so no one noticed her absence when the bus departed. She waited, but nothing changed. As sunset approached, she grew hungry. She saw a mango tree in the garden but found it too tall to reach. After many attempts, a mango finally fell, which she ate. Determined to find an escape, she searched around the campus. The compound wall was too high to scale, but she noticed a window in the principal's office, covered with tape. As she approached, the room's light turned on.

She found a hole near the gate that led to a hidden subway and decided to enter. This passage took her near the principal's office, an area she had never explored in her five years at the school. Cautiously, she approached and opened the door, but nothing seemed unusual inside, aside from an old telephone. Meanwhile, the students on the trip were enjoying themselves, unaware of Nithya's absence. Eventually, Vinothitha noticed her sister was missing. She became frantic, and the teachers on the trip assumed Nithya might have gone to the restroom and missed the bus, so they contacted the police.

At school, Nithya tried using the telephone but found it out of order. She took a torch and exited the subway, searching for a tool to break the lock. She found a gardening axe and tried to force the lock open but was exhausted. Just then, a woman walking nearby heard Nithya's call for help. With her husband's assistance, the woman helped Nithya out. Nithya then called her mother, who promptly came to pick her up. She also informed the teachers, putting everyone's worries to rest so they could continue enjoying the trip.

MORAL: Learn to say "no" and speak up boldly for yourself.

Author's Profile:

Shanthana, a creative student from IX, is passionate about both drawing and dancing, bringing energy and expression to everything she does. Known for her resilience and ability to accept and move forward in any situation, Shanthana possesses a maturity beyond her years. Her ambition to become an IAS officer reflects her commitment to making a positive impact. We are excited to see the paths she will forge and look forward to supporting her journey.

29

THE MYSTERY GAME

– MANOJ S V

Max and Jake were still trying to adjust to their new life in the old house. Everything felt different—like something was missing. Their parents had separated, and their mom had decided that moving to a new place would help them start fresh, but neither of them felt at home. The house was large and strange, full of dark corners and forgotten rooms.

One rainy afternoon, while they were exploring the basement, Max stumbled across something odd—an old, dusty box tucked away in a corner. It was a heavy metal, with strange symbols engraved on the surface. There was no name on it, just a symbol Max couldn't recognize. He didn't know what it was, but something about it intrigued him.

He carried it upstairs to show Jake, who was busy on his phone. "Hey, check this out!" Max said, setting the box down in front of him.

Jake barely looked up. "What is it now, another pointless game?" Max ignored him and opened the box. Inside was a board, a set of oddly shaped pieces, and a single die. The instructions were simple: "Place the pieces. Roll the die. Follow the instructions that appear." Jake groaned but reluctantly agreed to play. "This does not make sense, but whatever. You're responsible for managing this if it goes wrong."

Max set up the board, and they both sat down to play. Jake rolled the die, and they waited for something to happen. Nothing at first. But then, suddenly, the room seemed to tremble. The lights flickered, and the air around them grew thick. The game board began to glow, and before they could react, everything around them changed.

The walls of the living room disappeared. The floor beneath their feet was gone, replaced by a vast, swirling mist. The sky above was dark, and stars blinked far in the distance. They were floating in an endless void. Max and Jake stood frozen, the game board hovering between them. The next message on the board flashed: "Pirates of the Void. Lose a turn."

The Pirates of the Void Before they could react, a fleet of massive pirate ships appeared from the mist, their sails tattered, and their cannons aimed at them. The ships hovered in the space around them, their crews shouting commands in a strange, guttural language. Pirate ships weren't supposed to be real, yet here they were, closing in fast. Jake's eyes widened with fear. "What? We're in space! How is this happening?" Max grabbed his arm. "Look! We have to roll again. Maybe that will do something." But the next role only seemed to make things worse. As the die hit the board, a loud cannon blast sounded from one of the ships, narrowly missing them. Max and Jake ducked behind a nearby floating rock for cover.

The pirates began firing relentlessly at anything that moved, and the brothers realized they were in serious danger. "We need a plan," Max said, thinking quickly. "Maybe we can distract them?" Jake scowled but agreed. "Fine, you come up with something, genius." Max's eyes scanned the space around them. There were no escape routes, but he noticed a small asteroid floating nearby. "We can use that as a shield," he suggested. The brothers darted toward the asteroid, narrowly avoiding another cannon blast. They used it as cover while the pirates searched the area, eventually giving up the chase. "We got lucky," Jake muttered, panting. "But I think that's just the start." The Shifting Maze after the pirates were gone, the game board flickered again, and the next challenge appeared: "Shifting Maze. Make it to the center before time runs out." Suddenly, the space around them began to warp and twist.

The floating rock they had taken cover behind was now part of a giant maze—a vast labyrinth of walls made from shimmering light. Some walls were tall, others short, but every few seconds, they shifted, creating new paths and obstacles. The brothers tried to stay calm as the maze closed in on them. They could hear a loud ticking noise in the air, signaling that the walls would shift again soon. Max ran ahead, but Jake hesitated, eyeing the maze with a sense of dread. "Come on, we don't have much time!" Max called. The walls around them shifted again, cutting off their path. Max and Jake had to backtrack, finding new routes and jumping over obstacles as the maze became more complex.

It felt like every wrong turn led to a dead end, and time was running out.

Max noticed that the path ahead seemed to glow faintly, leading to the center of the maze. But the closer they got, the more the walls began to shift rapidly, trying to trap them. "I can't do this! It's impossible!" Jake shouted. But Max grabbed his hand. "Yes, you can. We just need to stick together." They both sprinted, using the glow of the center as their guide, leaping over walls just as they were about to close. With a final leap, they reached the center of the maze just as the walls locked into place, trapping them inside a glowing sphere. The game board flickered again.

"Next Challenge: Gravity Shift." The gravity shifted. The floor beneath them began to rumble, and the entire room seemed to tilt. Max felt himself being pulled toward the ceiling, and Jake shouted in surprise as he floated upward, his feet leaving the ground. The laws of gravity seemed to be completely flipped. "What's happening now?!" Jake yelled as he tried to push himself down, but it felt like he was swimming through the air. Max tried to steady himself, using the game board to anchor his movements. "I think the gravity's shifting. We need to stay close to the board and move carefully!" The floor tilted again, and soon they were both floating in mid-air, with objects and furniture floating around them like they were in zero gravity.

The boys had to use their arms to push off the walls and ceiling to avoid crashing into floating debris. They navigated their way to a corner, where the gravity finally stabilized, but they both felt disoriented. "This is insane!" Jake said, catching his breath. "How do we keep this up?" Max looked down at the game board again, where the next message appeared: "Final Challenge: Escape the Void." Escape the Void Max and Jake were finally nearing the game, but the final challenge was by far the most difficult. The room around them began to warp again, and an enormous vortex opened in the center of the space. It was pulling everything toward it—furniture, debris, even the stars themselves seemed to be sucked into the black hole.

"Get to the edge!" Max shouted, grabbing Jake's arm as the pull of the vortex grew stronger. The boys sprinted toward the edge of the room, but the closer they got, the stronger the pull. The walls began to crumble, and the floor was disappearing beneath their feet. Max could barely hold on, but with a final push, he and Jake reached the edge just as the vortex sucked the last of the room into the void. The game board flickered one last time, and the next message appeared: "Return Home." The room returned to normal in an instant, as if nothing had ever happened. The stars vanished, the gravity stabilized, and the game board was just an ordinary object again, sitting quietly on the coffee table.

Max and Jake were back in the living room, breathing heavily but alive. They looked at each other in silence for a moment. "Well," Jake said, wiping sweat from his forehead, "that was insane." Max smiled. "Yeah. But we did it." The game had tested them in ways they never imagined, but in, it brought them closer together. They both knew they would never forget what they had been through—and the way they had learned to trust each other along the way. As the sun began to set outside, Max glanced at the game one last time. "Do you think it could ever come back?" Jake shrugged. "Let's hope it doesn't. But I'm not so scared of it anymore."

Author's Profile:

Manoj of grade V is a responsible and mature student who demonstrates strong leadership skills. Manoj excels in managing and motivating others to achieve their best. In academics, he is highly talented, consistently producing strong results across subjects. His sense of humor and positive attitude make him a well-liked student, capable of lightening the atmosphere.

30

MIRA'S DREAM

– KAVINAYA M

Mira, a 7-year-old girl living with her grandparents, was sleeping peacefully in her room on a dark night. In her room, there was an old mirror that suddenly began to glow. Curious, Mira went closer and touched it, only to be pulled inside.

When Mira opened her eyes, she found herself in Chocolate Land. She was thrilled to see chocolates everywhere, but every time she tried to eat one, it disappeared. Feeling disappointed and hungry, she spotted the old mirror again. Hoping it would take her back home, she jumped inside.

This time, Mira arrived in a deep forest. She found some fruits and plucked them to eat. Just as she was enjoying the fruits, she heard a horrible noise, sending a chill down her spine. Not knowing what to do, she was relieved when the old mirror appeared once more. She quickly jumped inside.

Now, Mira found herself in Lava Land, where the heat was intense. It was unbearable, and she started crying. Right then, the mirror appeared again. She eagerly jumped inside, hoping to escape the scorching land.

The next place she found herself was Iceland, covered in frozen ice. Mira started to shiver as she had no slippers or boots. She couldn't stand on the ice, and suddenly, it began to crack under her feet. Terrified, she started running back and forth. Just then, the mirror appeared again, and Mira, relieved to see it, said, "Hey! You old mirror, you're back again!"

Desperate to escape, Mira jumped into the mirror once more. Now, she was in the ocean, sitting in a small fishing boat. She noticed a small hole in the boat, and water started leaking inside. As the boat began to sink, Mira clung to a piece of wood for safety. The mirror appeared yet again, and Mira prayed to be taken back home. She swam towards the mirror and jumped in.

This time, she landed in Fairyland, surrounded by beautiful fairies. Thinking they could help her, she approached them. But just as she was about to ask for help, she felt something wet. Someone was sprinkling water on her, it was her grandmother. At that moment, Mira realized that everything had just been a dream. She sighed with relief, knowing she was safe and sound at home.

Author's Profile:

Kavinaya, 11-year-old with a passion for storytelling, excels in narrating and crafting her own stories based on reality. A grade 6 student, she weaves intricate plots, exploring the power of dreams and imagination.

31

THE TALKING TREE

– ADHOKSHAJAA RAO. A

In a small village, there was a tree that everyone said was magical. It was big and old, with branches that stretched high into the sky. But the most amazing thing about this tree was that it could talk. One day, Arjun was playing near the tree, and suddenly, he heard a voice. "Hello, Arjun." He looked around, but no one was there. "Don't be afraid," said the tree. "I wanted to be your friend." Arjun was thrilled. He began talking to the tree as well. They became good friends. The tree shared stories and secrets of the forest. Every day, Arjun visited his new friend. They talked, laughed, and enjoyed the magic of nature together.

MORAL:

Nature is full of wonders and surprises. The magical tree symbolizes the beauty and mystery of the natural world. By forming a friendship with the tree, Arjun discovered the joy of connecting with nature and the importance of appreciating its gifts.

Author's Profile:

Adhokshajaa, a multi-talented grade 3 child who is an extrovert, who thrives on engaging in healthy conversations. He enjoys challenging himself by reading difficult words and exploring a wide range of books, which has helped him develop an impressive vocabulary and a love for learning.

32

MY DREAM: A JOURNEY TO THE WONDERLAND

– SAANVI C

As I lay down on my cozy bed, gazing at the glowing stars on the ceiling, I dozed off, only to wake up in a land far away, filled with wonders. Everywhere I looked, the world was filled with yummy chocolates: streetlights made of sugar candies, a lake filled with liquid chocolate, and a rowboat made of biscuits, with shrubs bearing muffins.

Seeing all these wonders made me excited, and I ran all around Wonderland. All of a sudden, it started raining—raining gems all over! I grabbed a few gems and started eating them slowly, one by one, as I sat under a tree. I looked up at the tree and was amazed to see that every branch bore a different flavour of Cadbury chocolate. I started counting all the Cadbury chocolates and fell asleep under the chocolate tree.

Suddenly, I woke up to the sight of a beautiful fairy standing in front of me. The fairy took me by the hand and led me to her huge castle. She made sure I was treated like a princess. I started walking around the castle, admiring all the wonderful artwork and architecture. I was delighted to be in the castle. As I walked around, I reached the farthest end of the castle and saw a huge door that opened to the sight of a beautiful beach. I ran to the beach and started playing there. All of a sudden, I saw a huge wave coming toward me. I was very afraid as the wave came closer, and I suddenly woke up, only to find that I had been dreaming all along.

This was my journey to Wonderland.

Author's Profile:

Saanvi (Grade IV) is a respectful, creative, and enthusiastic student who brings both talent and positivity to everything she does. She is always willing to help others and strives to make the most of every learning opportunity. Her imaginative ideas, along with her respectful and energetic nature, make her a joy to have in the classroom.

33

THE WORLD OF STUDIES VS THE WORLD OF SPORTS

– NIKAMANT KRISHNA G J

One fine day, the World split into two parts, studies, and sports. World studies have a sharp mind which makes them focused, the world of sports has a strong mind.

The world studies got harder they had busy lives and innovative projects. They do everything perfectly but there are problems. The first problem is "bully guys." They bully the person to make them tense and make them hesitate. The second problem is that the city is stuck in traffic very often. The cars are stuck in the road, they make the city polluted and look foggy.

In the sports world, they were fit and massive. Instead of milk, they drink health supplements. The problems were in football, the "small guys," scored a goal easily because the small guys were smaller than the fit guys.

Once there was a challenge on who can find the oldest rock on the earth. The sports world took the oldest rock from the museum. The world of studies had different machines in hand, they took their advantage and were mining till the earth looked like a step. They got the world's oldest rock, and it was giant like an octopus brain.

The judge was welcomed with due respect. After seeing it he chose the rock from the studies world as the oldest rock in the world. The leader of the studies world told the rock from you was serendipity. The sports world asked what the meaning of "Serendipity" is, and the world of studies told us to use our dictionary. They did not know what serendipity and it was hard for them.

Then both worlds were united to become one world. The studies and fitness came together. The studies world needs fitness, and the sports world needs studies.

MORAL: Studies and sports are equally important for our lives.

Author's Profile:

Nikamant Krishna of grade V is a dedicated and sincere student who consistently strives to excel in all areas. He approaches every task with a strong commitment to performing his best. His creativity and artistic skills shine through in his work, making him a standout in artistic pursuits. Academically, Nikamant is a high performer, demonstrating a keen understanding of his subjects. His all-around abilities and positive attitude make him a respected and valuable member of the school community.

CHARULEKHA S

HRIDHIK KANNAN VELAVAR

KAVINAYA M

VIDHYUTH SHADAMARSHAN A

I AM AN AUTHOR

ADHOKSHAJAA RAO A

RASHMI M

SHANTHANA SHRI T

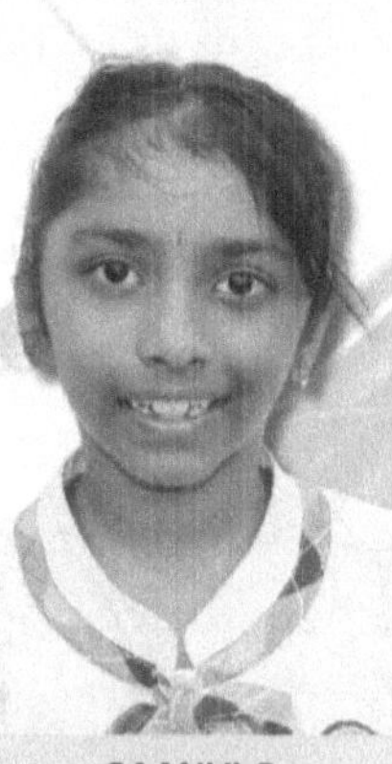

SAANVI C

SAMYUKTHA BASKARAN

MANOJ S V

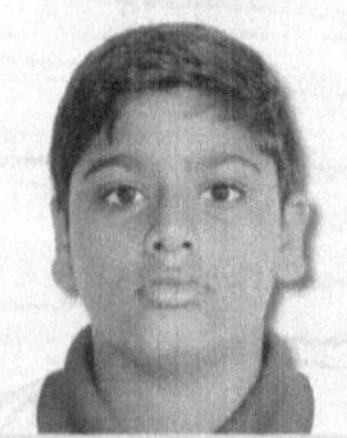

NIKAMANT KRISHNA G J

34

THE MAGICAL NECKLACES

– RAKSHATRIA L

Evelyn lived with her grandparents. Since her parents had to work out of town, she stayed with her grandparents for the day. Her grandparents asked her to clean the garage, which had been closed for years. While she was cleaning, she found a box. Curious, she opened it and found a pair of necklaces. She put one on and continued her work.

As she was talking to herself, she wished for the garage to be cleaned. To her amazement, her wish came true. Shocked, she went to her grandparents to explain what she had witnessed, but they didn't believe her. Determined to show them, she wished for a sandwich, but nothing happened.

Curious, she decided to try the other necklace. When she went to get it, however, it had disappeared. Instead, she found a letter near the box and started to read it. It said, "I have taken the necklace from the box. It was protected by a magical spell. Now that you have removed it, the spell is broken, and I can do anything with its power."

As she was walking, she accidentally dropped the letter in the water. When she picked up the wet letter, she noticed a hidden message: "If you want your necklace back, follow the black crystals." She grabbed her skateboard and started to follow the trail of black crystals without informing her grandparents. The crystals led her to an old factory.

Inside, she found a shiny mirror among some old clothes. She was amazed to see the shimmering mirror and remembered that the factory had been closed for years. She placed her hand in the mirror and was surprised to notice something hidden inside. Out of curiosity, she leaned closer, and the mirror pulled her inside. Evelyn was astonished to find herself in a different place.

She walked through this strange world until she reached an old castle, where she saw a demon holding the other necklace and a fairy trapped in a glass box in the corner. As she watched, the necklace began to glow, and suddenly, a powerful light flashed, turning the demon to ashes and freeing the fairy. The fairy thanked Evelyn and invited her to visit the castle whenever she wished.

Evelyn returned home, happy to have rescued the fairy. It had been a brave and adventurous day, one that gave her more courage to solve future mysteries.

Author's Profile:

Rakshatria of grade V is a responsible student who demonstrates strong leadership qualities both in and out of the classroom. Respected by her peers and teachers, she is known for her helpful nature and willingness to take on challenges. Whether assisting classmates with schoolwork or organizing group activities. Rakshatria is always ready to lend a hand and encourage others to succeed.

35

THE CASE OF MAGIC POTION

– ASHTON AROKIA RAJ

It was a bright sunny morning. The grass was still wet from the night dew. The twilight of the sun's rays makes the dew drops look like tiny sparkling diamonds. The chirping of the birds is no less than any pleasing music.

Alvin speaks into the walkie-talkie: "Hey Eva! Good morning! We have got cases to solve. Let's meet in my home backyard by 10:00 a.m., and yeah, don't forget to bring our detective kit. "Sure, Alvin. I am very excited to work on our new cases. See you at 10," says Eva.

Alvin and Eva, a 10-year-old, have been best friends since kindergarten and share the same neighborhood. They study at the same school and play together. Of course, they solve mystery cases together. Neighbors call them "The Detective Duos." Both are proud of their nicknames. It's their school year-end break, so no school, no homework, just busy with their mystery-solving cases.

Soon after breakfast, Eva geared up with all her detective stuff and rushed to Alvin's home. Both reached their favourite spot. It's a cubby house designed like a detective's office with equipment like a walkie-talkie, magnifying glasses, torch, boots, notepad, and pen. Alvin and Eva would spend hours together in their detective office discussing solving mystery cases.

Mysteries happening around

"Okay! Alvin, I am all ears, tell me what happened" says Eva. Alvin began to narrate the incidents that had been happening around for a few days in the town. "There has been a missing wallet from Mr. Walter's house, a missing ferret from our friend Leo's house, and a missing backpack from Ashley's house," says Alvin. Eva was shocked to hear so many missing cases in their town for the past few days.

Alvin and Eva planned to start the investigation of cases one by one. They picked up their investigation stuff, and kits and headed right away to Mr. Walter's house.

The hunt begins

Mr. Walter is an old gentleman in the town. He is an active 80-year-old, who lives alone in his house. Eva greeted Mr. Walter and started shooting out her questions. So, here are the few facts Eva has gathered in the case. Mr. Walter was watching television after he came home from shopping. He has kept his wallet on the table beside him, which he is 100% sure of. To his surprise all of a sudden, his wallet disappeared. There was no trace of someone breaking into the house. Alvin and Eva left Mr. Walter's house in vain as they couldn't gather any lead for the missing wallet.

Next, they visited their friend from school Leo's house. Leo is a pet lover and is very attached to his ferret, which he got as a gift from his dad for his birthday. Leo said that his ferret Molly was playing a fetch ball game with him. When Leo had gone to fetch the ball, in a jiffy moment his ferret had gone missing. Alvin began to search the entire house with his magnifying glass to check for the footprint. Once again, their search had gone in vain. Both left Leo's house with a sad face and headed to Ashley's house.

Alvin and Eva were distressed to hear the same kind of story from Ashley too. All three possessions of the town residents had gone missing right in front of them. Alvin and Eva strongly believed that there could be some connection between these three cases.

Getting closer

On their way back to the detective's office, Alvin and Eva noticed something odd. A group of young kids were gathered around an old, abandoned house. The house was abandoned for ages, and no one lived there. Alvin and Eva went to enquire about this to the kids. As soon as the kids saw the detectives, they ran away in all directions out of fear. "Something is not right," said Alvin. "Let's go home and come back again later in the evening," said Eva.

As the sun went down, Alvin and Eva gathered their stuff, with their headlights on, and tried to sneak into the abandoned house to see if anything was going on. They were so quiet in their mission. Eva slowly opened the main door, and they entered inside. The house was pitch dark. Both could sense some pungent smell inside the house. "Phew, what a nasty smell," said Alvin. Eva signaled Alvin to be quiet.

There was a room inside the house, the door of the room was closed with little open, both could see dim light inside the room. Slowly, Eva opened the door. Alvin and Eva were horrified to see an old man doing some kind of experiments with colored liquids. The room looked more like their chemistry lab. Both could sense that the old person was doing some kind of illegal work there. The old man was busy with his work and hardly noticed the two kids watching him.

Alvin and Eva quietly ran away from the place and planned to bring all the elderly people from the town. Soon they informed their parents and other people in town. Everyone gathered along with Alvin and Eva and planned to confront the old man about his experiments.

The "Magic Potion"

Upon enquiring, the old man admitted that he was creating a "Magic Potion" which could make you invisible for some time after drinking it. Alvin and Eva understood that the old man had given the magic potion to the kids in town and made them steal things from him. The old man further said that the magic potion was still in the testing stage and wanted to try it on someone else before he could use it for himself. In this way, the old man thought that he could steal other people's stuff and become rich. The townspeople immediately called the police and handed over the old man to them as he was doing illegal activities and misusing kids for his work.

The old man was arrested by police, and they recovered all the missing items of people in the town from him. Police and town residents thanked Alvin and Eva for their brave and bold help in finding the person behind the missing things.

Alvin and Eva were super proud of their work and left home happily, and of course, they were ready to solve the next mystery case.

MORAL: You can't escape from the evil problems you have created.

Author's Profile:

Ashton Arokia Raj of grade V is a talented student who excels in both academic and extracurricular activities. His quick wit and sense of humor make him a fun and engaging individual. Ashton's energetic personality ensures he's always enthusiastic about taking on new challenges and contributing ideas, making him a valuable team member.

36

MYSTERY OF MILTON

– TRISHNA KRISHIKA BALAN

Milton was located somewhere in Australia. Even though it was centrally located, not many people lived there. Many reasons are speculated for its infamous difference. It all started when a group of people came across the ocean, fighting for their lives. These people had lived happily on an island located somewhere in the middle of the ocean. However, when a great tsunami washed over and swallowed their home, they fled to Australia. They were religious people, with many cultural worships and duties. But after shifting to this new land, they feared that their devils would harm them and that gods would punish them. But this was just one problem.

As every other day went by, the people continued their usual work. But that very night, they knew they were doomed. That night, a perfectly healthy young man died for a reason no one knew. From that very same day, every night a single young man would die. Fearing for their lives, many young men, along with their families, fled the town of Milton, and all those who fled survived. And all of this is perfectly true, as it was recorded in many places.

Now, there are several theories addressing this mystery. Some suggest poisoning, others mention toxic gases, but these were not possible. After all, why were only young men harmed, and why only at night? Their bodies would shake vigorously, their mouths would unusually froth, and before anyone knew it, they would die.

After years of research and trials, the concluded theory is that it had something to do with nightmares. Since these people were from another place, they were scared, as everything was new to them, including the language and the area. The men were terrified of their religious monsters, and they faced nightmares. The nightmares were so intense that the men suffered cardiac arrest and died in their sleep.

But it still remains a mystery why this happened only to young men and why it occurred only in the town of Milton. Luckily, this horror is no more. It remains a famous medical mystery and will always remain a mystery...

Author's Profile:

Trishna, a grade VII student and passionate reader of fiction, has developed a flair for creating thrilling mystery stories. Inspired by her favourite novels, she crafts complex plots full of suspense and intrigue, showcasing her unique storytelling skills.

37

THE GOLDEN HEIST

– AADHESH J. K

Prologue

The city of Glenwood was known for its golden allure. Sunlight seemed to linger just a bit longer on its cobblestone streets, casting a warm glow over its historic buildings and bustling marketplaces. But beneath these gilded exteriors lay secrets as cold and hard as stone—secrets that drew the interest of Detective Charles Higgins, a rookie investigator with a reputation for persistence.

Higgins had only recently joined the ranks of the city's detectives, but his sharp instincts and relentless curiosity set him apart. Eager to prove himself, he took on every case, big or small, with a tenacity that sometimes earned him more skeptical looks than praise. But the thrill of uncovering the truth, of peeling back layers others overlooked, kept him moving forward.

Little did he know that today, his unassuming stroll down Main Street would change his career forever, propelling him into a case that would test every skill he had—and reveal just how deep greed could run, even in a place that glittered like Glenwood.

STORY

One day, as Detective Higgins strolled down the bustling main street, he was startled by a loud crash echoing through nearby alleyways. Intrigued, he followed the sound, weaving through the crowd, until he arrived at the source: a gold shop with shattered glass scattered across the pavement. The shop's elegant sign—engraved with delicate gold leaf—now hung askew, a stark contrast to the broken storefront. Through the fractured glass, sunlight glinted off scattered jewelry and fragments of display cases strewn across the plush, red-carpeted floor. Inside, customers and staff stood frozen in shock, their faces pale and wide-eyed.

Upon entering, Higgins noticed a small sign by the door: "Please remove your shoes." He slipped off his shoes respectfully and stepped inside. The shop was filled with the scent of polished wood and velvet. Behind the counter, an elderly man sat in distress, his hands trembling as he pressed them to his face. His red-rimmed eyes met Higgins's, and he whispered, "They took everything…"

Higgins introduced himself and offered to investigate, and the shop owner, hopeful for any help, quickly agreed. Higgins began his investigation by questioning the employees, who described the terrifying ordeal: "There were three men. One pointed a gun at us, another gathered up the gold, and a third waited outside in a getaway car." Higgins observed the scene, his gaze catching a small, glinting piece of gold nestled in a dusty footprint. He carefully collected a sample of the dust and sent it to the forensic team.

The results returned almost immediately, revealing an unexpected lead—the dust matched minerals found near Mt. Rushmore. Higgins set off toward the area, driving through the countryside until he reached a dense, forested mountain range. The air was crisp, filled with the sharp scent of pine, and as Higgins followed a narrow trail, he soon spotted an abandoned factory hidden among the towering trees.

The factory was vast and eerie, its walls streaked with rust and ivy. Cracked windows revealed empty, shadowed rooms, and silence filled the space as he stepped inside. In a small office at the back, he froze at the sight before him—a large, gleaming lump of gold lying untouched on a dusty table.

As he approached, there was a sudden clang as the doors slammed shut, locking him inside. Startled, he scanned the dim room and found a small, crumpled piece of paper near the door. It contained a cryptic list of dates:

3rd of August

1st of October

3rd of July

1st of December

4th of November

1st of November

Keeping the riddle in mind, he found a way out and soon spotted two men fleeing through the forest. Drawing his pistol, he called out, "Stop!" Startled, they froze, and as he approached, they confessed, revealing that the mastermind behind it all was none other than the gold shop owner.

Back in the city, Higgins led a police team to the shop owner's grand mansion. The estate, surrounded by wrought-iron gates and lush gardens, was a striking picture of wealth and prestige. The house itself was grand, with vaulted ceilings, ornate chandeliers, and walls lined with gilded mirrors and paintings. When the shop owner opened the door and saw Higgins with the two captured men, his face paled.

At first, he denied everything, but as the weight of evidence pressed in on him, he slumped in defeat and confessed. Drowning in debt, he had orchestrated the robbery to claim a large insurance payout while secretly keeping some of the gold stashed away.

But Higgins had one more question for him. "If you wanted to get away with this, why did you allow me to investigate? You could've turned me away."

The shop owner gave a bitter chuckle. "You're just a rookie. I thought you'd never solve it… Thought you'd get tangled in the details and give up. Guess I was wrong."

With the truth revealed Higgins reported every detail to his agency. His boss, thoroughly impressed, asked, "And how did you solve that riddle?"

Higgins explained the dates and the key to unlocking the door.

"I realized each date hinted at a specific letter," he explained.

- 3rd of August gave the 3rd letter: **G**
- 1st of October gave the 1st letter: **O**
- 3rd of July gave the 3rd letter: **L**
- 1st of December gave the 1st letter: **D**
- 4th of November gave the 4th letter: **E**
- 1st of November gave the 1st letter: **N**

"All together, it spelled out 'GOLDEN.' That word unlocked the door—and pointed me to the truth."

His boss nodded, thoroughly impressed. "Brilliant work, Higgins."

From that day on, Higgins's reputation as one of the city's most promising detectives was solidified, his sharp instincts proving that rookies could indeed solve the toughest cases.

Author's Profile:

Aadhesh J. K., a spirited student from grade IX, brings excitement and curiosity to all his interests. An avid cricket player, he enjoys the thrill of the game as much as the intrigue of a great story. Aadhesh loves adventure movies and draws inspiration from the mysteries of Sherlock Holmes, fueling his imaginative thinking. With a passion for unravelling puzzles and seeking new adventures, Aadhesh's creativity shines in his storytelling.

38

THE LOST FILE

– AKANKSHA DAS

Leena a diligent journalist, sat at her desk, going through the latest news about the string of mysterious disappearances throughout the city, while sipping her lukewarm coffee. Suddenly her phone beeped signaling a message, she found it to be from an unknown number. *"Meet me at the old tower at midnight"*, the message read, *"Come alone"*. Her instincts said her to be cautious, and not to go, but curiosity took over her. She finally decided to go over to the tower…. alone.

At midnight she approached the old tower, the mist and the darkness, making it hard to see, however the moon's light glistening onto the city made it look euphoric. Leena was lost admiring the beauty of the city, forgetting everything. Suddenly a figure emerged from the shadows – a hooded woman. Who looked like she knew about what Leena was searching for the answers to it. Suddenly she took something out of her pocket, Leena became conscious and was ready if she was going to attack. But she said something…. Unexpected.

"You're looking for answers," the woman said, handing Lena a small USB drive. "This contains the file you need." Leena seemed confused about what she was talking about, yet she took the USB, hesitating. The woman vanished into the night, leaving Lena with more questions than answers

Once she got back home, she plugged the drive into her laptop, and a single document opened: "Project Elysium: Mind Control Experimentation"

Chills ran down her spine as she scrolled through the disturbing contents.

As Lena delved deeper into the file, she realized she was being watched. Yet she kept on reading when suddenly, her laptop screen flickered, and a message appeared: "You shouldn't have looked." She was confused, but more scared she sat there in silence, wondering about what the message meant. Lena's phone rang, shrill in the silence. It was her editor, Mark. "Leena, we've received a tip about a mindblower at the city's medical research center. Investigate and get back to me." Leena, though scared, couldn't refuse and had to go, as this is the only chance she could get about the case.

Lena arrived at the research center, her heart racing. Inside, she met Dr. Rachel Kim, a brilliant neuroscientist with a guarded expression. Looking at her face she knew that Dr. Kim definitely knew something about the case, so she was the first to be investigated. "What do you know about Project Elysium?" Lena asked.

Dr. Kim glanced around nervously and hesitated for a minute before answering, "It's a clandestine operation. They're experimenting with mind control, manipulating memories... I've seen terrible things." She took a pause but when she was about to continue, a loud noise echoed down the hallway.

"We need to leave, now," Dr. Kim urged, her face had turned pale and, as they fled, Lena realized she was in grave danger. As they were running, a tall, brooding figure appeared: "I'm Ethan, a former Elysium operator. I've been watching you, Lena. You're getting close to the truth." His face was emotionless, and dark circles were around his eyes as if he hadn't slept for days.

Ethan's eyes locked onto Dr. Kim. "You're the one who helped me escape."

Dr. Kim nodded. "I had to. You were the only one who could expose the truth."

Lena's mind looked for answers to the questions; What secrets did Ethan hold?

Would Dr. Kim's expertise be enough to unravel the mystery? And who was behind Project Elysium? Both noticed the confusion in Leena's eyes and asked them to follow him, he took them to a safe house and that's where Ethan revealed his past.

"I was recruited for Elysium's mind control program. They erased my memories and programmed me to obey. But Dr. Kim helped me break free." What is Elysium's mind control program" asked Leena. Dr. Kim explained: "Project Elysium aims to create super-soldiers, controlled by the government. They're using civilians as test subjects, manipulating memories to create false realities".

Lena's eyes widened. "That's the same Governor who's been pushing for increased surveillance and control." Dr. Kim nodded. "It's all connected. Elysium is just the tip of the iceberg."

With Ethan's testimony and Dr. Kim's evidence, Lena wrote an explosive expose that could save many lives. She was awake the rest of the night and dint take any rest, as soon as she was done writing the story she rushed towards the headquarters, to publish the story as soon as possible. Once the story was released, it went viral, sparking outrage and demands for accountability. Governor Reed was arrested, and Project Elysium was shut down. Lena, Ethan, and Dr. Kim became heroes, hailed for their bravery.

As Lena reflected on the journey, she realized: "The truth is often hidden, but with courage, determination, and integrity, it can be revealed."

Author's Profile:

Akanksha Das, an excellent academician from IX std. She likes dance and is a good orator. She has good leadership qualities, and she is always an active participant in various activities. However, her writing reflects her creativity and critical thinking. She is a passionate reader and was inspired to write this story from Sydney Sheldon.

39

DETECTIVE ACE-MYSTERY OF THE THIEF

– AJEY SRIVANTH.N

It was a sunny, beautiful day in Cornerstone Town. Ace, a clever 14-year-old, was walking down the road, observing everything around him. You see, Ace wasn't just any boy – he had a sharp mind, as you're about to discover.

While passing a beggar, Ace dropped a coin into his cup and then paused. "That's a pretty bad undercover operation you've got going," Ace said with a grin.

"Excuse me?" replied the "beggar," looking startled – and suspiciously like a police officer.

"You're a cop!" Ace declared.

"How did you figure that out?" asked the officer, surprised.

"Simple," Ace replied confidently. "First, you didn't thank me for the coin – most people in your position would. You look frustrated, and your posture suggests a backache. But the biggest clue? The earpiece you keep touching and your 'partner' over there, with the shape of his gun clearly visible under his shirt."

As Ace turned to leave, the officer, whose name was Mark, called after him. "Do you think you're smart?"

"Smart?" Ace shrugged. "Smart is boring. I'm just sharp. What case are you trying to solve?"

Mark sighed, hesitant but impressed. "We're looking for a thief who's been troubling the town."

Ace chuckled. "Why didn't you ask me sooner? I already know who the thief is. See that pregnant woman and her husband over there?"

Mark looked in the direction Ace pointed. "Yes...?"

"That woman is the thief. The 'bump' on her stomach? It's the goods she's stolen."

Acting on Ace's insight, the police quickly arrested the couple. Amazed, Mark asked, "How did you know?"

Ace smiled. "Just my sharp mind at work."

Author's Profile:

Ajey of grade IV is a smart child, wanting to be more social and loves collecting coins of different countries and ages too. He expresses his quest for knowledge by asking unconditional questions. He is a great artist who enjoys drawing which enhances his concentration and has motivated him to write the story.

40

FROM SHADOWS TO LIGHT

– PRANESH B V

Amma was a teacher, a warrior in every sense of the word. Though one of her eyes had fallen silent to blindness, her vision of life remained sharp and focused. Even after enduring the challenges of a severe COVID attack, she emerged stronger and more determined. Her greatest joy came twelve years ago when she gave birth to a precious gem of a son, Pranesh BV, in whom she saw endless possibilities.

Amma's strength was drawn from the unwavering support of her husband, who stood as her pillar through every storm. Together, they cultivated a home of resilience and warmth, one where challenges were mere stepping stones to success. Pranesh BV, growing up in this atmosphere of love and positivity, blossomed into a young boy with a mind full of dreams. His thoughts danced on paper, weaving stories of hope and triumph.

Now, at twelve, he was poised to become a young author, a pride not only to his parents but to all who knew him. Amma watched with pride as the darkness she once faced gave way to the light of her son's achievements. The struggles of the past were distant memories, overshadowed by the brightness of their present.

Amma's journey proved that no obstacle could dim the radiance of determination and love. Her story, and Pranesh BV's rise, were a testament to how darkness can be transformed into brilliance when fuelled by the unwavering power of family.

"UNSTOPPABLE POWER = AMMA"

Author's Profile:

Pranesh B V, an 11-year-old in Grade VI, is passionate about solving chess puzzles and making checkmates. He loves cricket, particularly bowling as a right-handed pace bowler, and enjoys playing tennis. Family is his top priority, and his love for them is his greatest addiction.

41

JANTUS AND HIS ADVENTURE IN THE SEA

– SAANVI C

Jantus was a lively little boy who lived in a village by the sea. His father, along with the other men in the village, used to go fishing every day. They would catch fish, bring it from the sea to the market, and sell their catch. This was their daily routine. Jantus, along with his friends, would play along the seashore every day.

One day, while Jantus was playing with his friends, a huge wave came towards them. The wave was so strong that Jantus was not able to run away, while his friends were far from the shore.

All his friends were really scared to go near the shore after seeing the huge wave take Jantus with it. Jantus tried to swim, but he grew tired and began to drown. He clung to a wooden log that came near him. The log drifted with the current. Jantus became unconscious.

He woke up suddenly. It was dark, and he could not see anything around him, but he could hear the sound of water.

He thought he could try to get help in the morning since he could not see anything around him. He dozed off to sleep again.

He woke up to the sharp rays of the sun falling on his face. He opened his eyes and saw that he was on a small island. He could see sand around him, with a few rocks. He took a rock and threw it on the sand. Suddenly, he felt the land shaking. He was afraid, but suddenly, water started shooting from the sand, and the island began to move. He realized it was not an island, but he was on the back of a huge dolphin. He clung to the dolphin's fin as it started swimming. He saw lots of smaller dolphins swimming around the big dolphin.

The dolphins kept swimming for a long time, and Jantus didn't know what to do or where they were going. But then, he saw land in the distance. He was relieved to see the shore nearing him. As the dolphins continued swimming, he could see the huts of his village. Finally, the dolphins came near the shore.

Jantus jumped from the dolphin and started swimming toward the shore. He was very happy to be alive and ran back to his village. He started telling his parents and friends what had happened the previous night. To his parents and friends, this was Jantus's adventure in the sea, far from land.

Author's Profile:

Saanvi (Grade IV) is a respectful, creative, and enthusiastic student who brings both talent and positivity to everything she does. She is always willing to help others and strives to make the most of every learning opportunity. Her imaginative ideas, along with her respectful and energetic nature, make her a joy to have in the classroom

42

THE LOST DOG AND THE FAMILY

– HARSHAVARDHAN S

Once upon a time, there was a dog named Rocky. He was born on 5th December 2015 in Madurai, the city of temples. Rocky was adopted by a loving family with four members. He was the fifteenth member of the family. All these family members lived in a chilly city called Hosur. Rocky was taken care of well by all the family members. He was very happy, protective, and very loyal to his family members.

But Rocky had a major health problem which was not identified by anyone. As the days were moving on happily. After a few years, when he was 5 years old, one of the family members got another dog called Simba. He was a very naughty doggy. Rocky was older than Simba. He did not like another member's entry into the family; Rocky was very possessive. So, both the dogs were kept at a distance. But the little naughty Simba was playful and got attached close to the family.

Rocky went into depression; he did not have his food properly. One day he left home, and everyone in the family was sad and searching for the dog all around the place.

After a few months, Rocky was found sick, and his health issue was very severe. Doctors said that he was suffering from liver failure. Medicine did not help him to recover his health. It was the last day for him, he took his last breath and died. The family members missed the lovable Rocky with hard hearts and tears. But he is still alive in the hearts of everyone in the family, including Simba.

MISS YOU ROCKY!

Author's Profile:

Harshavardhan of grade V is a creative student who enjoys exploring new ideas and thinking outside the box. His adventurous spirit often leads him to take on new challenges, both in academics and in his hobbies. While he may be shy, he excels in his work with a quiet skillfulness that draws attention to the quality of his contributions.

43

THE TIME TRAVELLING PENCIL

– SAMSKRITI R

One day, a girl named Shami was going through the drawers in her home to find her drawing pencils. She was searching for a long time until she had a thought to give up. Then unexpectedly a pencil fell out of a box she was about to throw out. She was also about to throw this pencil out until she realized it looked similar to her pencils, golden lines, a fake gem at but what made this pencil a bit weird was its lead. It almost looked like the pencil had a light at its tip. She didn't think much of it. She took out her sketch book and started to draw using this pencil. The first thing she drew was a knight with a huge sword. Right as she finished, everything started spinning! When Shami opened her eyes, she wasn't in her room anymore. She was in a real-life castle!

Just then, a young knight nearby was struggling to pick up his sword. Shami walked over and said, "Hey, maybe hold it like this." The knight tried, and it worked! "Thanks, kid!" the knight said with a smile. Shami thanked the knight back, feeling awestruck. Then, Shami thought about pirates. She picked up the magic pencil and quickly drew a pirate ship with sails and a flag. Baam! Suddenly, she was on a ship! The sea was super blue, and the captain handed her a map with a big red X. "Go find the treasure, matey!" the captain said. Shami replied " Aye - Aye Captain!!."Shami followed the map and found a chest filled with gold coins and sparkly jewels. But even though all this was amazing, she missed home. So, she grabbed the pencil one last time and quickly drew her own house.

And Whoosh...! Shami was back in her house, safe. She kept the magic pencil on her desk, disguising it, looking just like any other pencil. Shami smiled and whispered to the pencil, "Can't wait to go on another adventure with u.!!"

Author's Profile:

Samskrithi, (Grade VIII) a creative young writer, is the author of Time Travelling Pencil. Her story takes readers on a fascinating journey through different eras, blending imagination with adventure. Through this unique concept, Samskrithi explores the wonders and challenges of time travel in a playful yet thought-provoking way. Her narrative captures readers' curiosity, making each twist in the tale an exciting discovery.

44

THE CONUNDRUM'S EDGE

– SHAGANA S

"Today's class will push your minds beyond their usual boundaries," says Mrs. Cartney, the new philosophy teacher at the high school. She's leading a discussion on paradoxes—situations that seem self-contradictory yet may contain hidden truths. Axel Cipher, one of the most perceptive students in the class, finds the session especially captivating. Axel is an 18-year-old with a curious mind, particularly intrigued by the concept of time. Mrs. Cartney assigns a unique homework task that soon makes Axel's life feel suspenseful and filled with oddities. She tasks him with solving the "grandfather paradox," a scenario where someone travels back in time to harm their grandfather, raising questions about their own existence.

This challenge feels like a personal quest to Axel, who has always admired the mysteries of time. Later, during art class, he notices something unusual—his teacher is dressed in a neck corset, clawed gloves, and has styled her hair with bubble braids. Her lesson deviates from her usual topics, instead focusing on how time is designed in this world. Axel finds this strange, given her previous straightforward teaching style and ordinary attire.

After a half-decent dinner at home, Axel goes to bed as his mother gives him a warm, reassuring smile. Soon, he dreams of a girl with goat-like pupils, white lashes, a neck corset, and a long, bionic arm.

At first, Axel thinks he's in an imaginative dream, but he quickly realizes he's in a multiverse filled with characters that seem drawn from stories. The girl, who introduces herself as Aurora Kenesis, explains her unique ability to control the aurora lights. Axel glances up to find himself under the shimmering Northern Lights. With a flourish, Aurora begins manipulating the lights, creating a visual art display. In the display, Axel sees a version of himself in the future, using a time machine to journey to the past. But he doesn't look ordinary—instead, he has glowing nails, a single gray streak in his hair, petal-like eyelashes, and a perpetual smile. He appears more like a mythical figure than his usual self. In the vision, he sees himself travel back to when his grandfather was young, ending his life.

As the aurora lights shift, they form a new timeline. "That's it!" Axel exclaims, waking with excitement.

The next morning, Axel heads to school, convinced that all time-based paradoxes create alternate timelines that prevent conflicts with the present. In class, he's startled to see Mrs. Cartney speaking to someone with a gray streak in her hair and white lashes. Mrs. Cartney then announces an upcoming trip to see the Northern Lights and explore their connection with the multiverse, where they'll meet a mysterious figure named Aurora Kenesis.

Author's Profile:

Shagana, a curious and insightful student from grade IX, has a passion for reading fictional and paradox-based stories that challenge the boundaries of reality. Recently, she crafted an intriguing time-based paradox story, showcasing her unique storytelling abilities. In addition to her love for literature, Shagana has a keen interest in the stock market and trading, adding depth to her analytical skills. With a mind for both logic and imagination, Shagana's work promises to engage and inspire.

RAKSHATRIA L

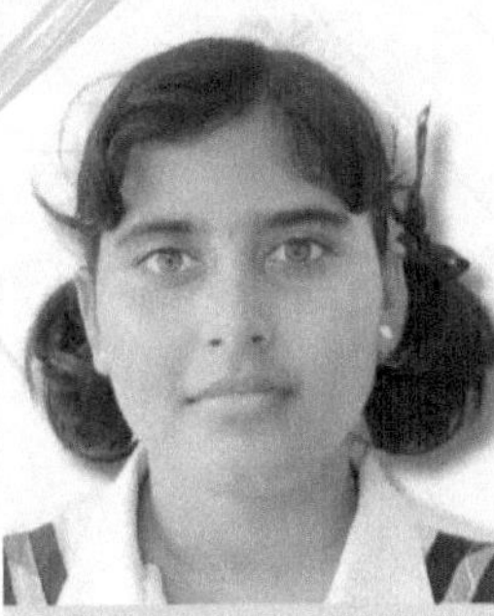

AKANKSHA DAS

SAANVI C

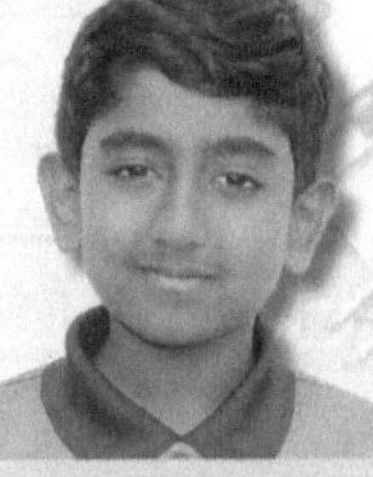

ASHTON AROKIA RAJ

I AM AN AUTHOR

M S DHONI
GLOBAL SCHOOL

HARSHAVARDHAN S

TRISHNA KRISHIKA BALAN

AJEY SRIVANTH N

SAMSKRITI R

AADHESH J K

PRANESH B V

SHAGANA S

45

THE ERA OF SHADOWS

– MRIDHUL GIRI

In a future where the boundaries of memory had been shattered, Dr. Jessica Renfield's invention—the Miayoka and its device, the Supreme—promised a world of shared experiences and heightened understanding. But when a shadowy figure infiltrated the Nexus and stole the Supreme's data, everything changed. What began as a technological marvel spiraled into a decade of chaos and crime, as the Miayoka's power fell into the wrong hands.

The world descended into an era marked by violence, theft, and manipulation. Criminal syndicates emerged, using the Miayoka to implant false memories, erase identities, and turn people into unwitting pawns in their schemes. The courts were overwhelmed, unable to keep up with the tide of deceit and lawlessness. Justice became a rare commodity, and fear gripped cities worldwide.

Recognizing the dire situation, a coalition of nations gathered to address the escalating crisis. They understood that traditional law enforcement was inadequate to tackle this new breed of crime. What they needed was an elite task force—individuals who possessed not only courage and skill but also an understanding of the intricacies of memory manipulation. Thus, the Mavericks were born.

The Mavericks were selected from the best of the best—detectives, hackers, psychologists, and former military operatives, each with a unique skill set. They underwent rigorous training in a hidden facility designed to simulate memory manipulation scenarios. Under the leadership of Jessica, who had been brought back into the fold despite her guilt over the Miayoka's misuse, the Mavericks prepared to confront the looming shadows of injustice.

Jessica watched as the team trained, her heart heavy with the knowledge of what her invention had unleashed. "We have to outsmart the criminals," she said during their first briefing. "They know how to manipulate memories. We need to learn how to see through their lies and reclaim the truth."

The team consisted of:

Ryder, a former intelligence officer with a knack for reading people.

Sophie, a brilliant hacker who could exploit the very networks criminals used to hide their activities.

Liam, a psychologist who specialized in memory recovery and manipulation.

Nina, a skilled combatant and strategist, trained in various martial arts.

Their first mission came quickly. Reports had surfaced about a notorious crime syndicate known as The Specters, who had begun using Miayoka technology to erase the memories of witnesses, leaving them confused and unable to testify against their leaders. The Mavericks knew they had to move fast.

As they infiltrated the criminal underworld, using Sophie's hacking skills to gather intel, they discovered that The Specters were planning a major operation—a mass memory heist that would cripple the city's law enforcement.

On the night of the operation, the Mavericks set a trap. They followed the trail to an abandoned warehouse on the outskirts of the city. As they entered, the air thick with tension, they found themselves in a vast room filled with makeshift equipment and stolen data from the Supreme.

Suddenly, the lights flickered, and the leader of The Specters, a figure known only as **Shade**, emerged from the shadows, flanked by armed henchmen. "You're too late, Mavericks," he sneered, a twisted smile on his face. "Tonight, we rewrite reality!"

The Mavericks sprang into action. Ryder focused on distracting Shade, drawing his attention with calculated taunts. Meanwhile, Liam used his expertise to analyze the memory devices scattered throughout the warehouse, identifying which ones were capable of erasing memories.

As the chaos erupted, Sophie worked furiously to hack into the system, disabling security protocols while Nina engaged the henchmen in hand-to-hand combat. The fight was fierce, but the Mavericks had trained for this moment.

In a crucial moment, Jessica, who had been monitoring from a safe distance, realized the data was about to be wiped clean. She sprinted toward the main console, shouting, "Sophie, I need you to create a diversion!"

Sophie nodded, initiating a feedback loop in the security system that sent sparks flying and caused the lights to blink erratically. In the confusion, Jessica accessed the core memory drives, determined to download the data before it was lost.

Just as she finished, Shade lunged at her, but Nina intercepted him, delivering a powerful kick that sent him sprawling. "Go! We'll hold them off!" Nina shouted.

With the data secure, Jessica rejoined the team, and together they managed to subdue the remaining henchmen. As Shade was captured, the Mavericks finally felt a sense of victory. They had thwarted the heist and uncovered vital information about the wider network of criminal activities that spanned the globe.

In the aftermath, the data from the Supreme was integrated into a new system designed to restore erased memories and protect witnesses from manipulation. The Mavericks became a symbol of hope, proving that justice could be reclaimed even in an age of shadows.

As the years rolled on, the team continued to combat the rising tide of crime, restoring integrity to a world that had nearly lost its way. Jessica, though still haunted by the past, found purpose in the work of the Mavericks. They were the guardians of memory, ensuring that the Miayoka was used not as a weapon of chaos but as a tool for healing and understanding.

The era of shadows was far from over, but with the Mavericks on the front lines, the light of justice flickered defiantly against the darkness, promising a future where memories—and the truth—could finally be safeguarded.

BUT IS THE CRIMINAL (THIEF) STILL FOUND? THE STORY OF THE MAVERICKS CONTINUES...

Author's Profile:

Mridhul Giri, a creative and imaginative Grade VIII student, is the author of The Era of Shadows. With a keen interest in science fiction and futuristic themes, Mridhul explores complex ideas of memory, technology, and justice in his storytelling. His narrative skills bring to life suspenseful scenes and thought-provoking questions about society and humanity. Mridhul's passion for writing shines through his captivating and insightful work.

46

THE RACE

– DEVAPRYAG SHYAM

Once there was a car named Skull Breaker. It was the fastest car in the world. One day The Skull Breaker's engine suddenly stopped in the middle of the racetrack, and it had to be towed away to the garage for repairs. When the mechanics declared that the Skull Breaker could not be repaired its owner moved it into the junkyard where the Skull Breaker was left to rust.

After several months of neglect, the Skull Breaker was in a state of despair, during one stormy night the Skull Breaker came to life after being struck by lightning. The skull breaker now started searching for metal objects which would make him more powerful.

There was one man named Aalparambil Gopi whose car's metal parts were stolen by the Skull Breaker. So, he and his friend Malgosh KP went and met the Chief Minister requesting him to revive the World Cup so that the Skull Breaker could also participate. The Chief Minister agreed, and the race was announced. The Skull Breaker was invited to participate in the race.

The contestants of the race were Gopi, Malgosh, Lal, and Ravana Prabhu. Alparambil Gopi was driving a Jaguar with a V8 Engine, Malgosh was driving a Swift, Ravana Prabhu was driving a Tata Nexon, and Lal was using an I20.

The race began as planned but it started raining Lal was the first one to get disqualified from the race as his car skidded from the racetrack. The skull breaker was able to beat the other race cars quite easily. The first obstacle was Half Roads where there was no paved racetrack for several meters. The skull breaker cleared that easily by doing a 360-degree flip. Gopi, Ravana Prabhu, and Malgosh cleared the obstacle with difficulty.

The last obstacle in the race was the Mushroom Tunnel where the cars had to cross without bouncing. Gopi, Ravan Prabu, and Malgosh were driving too fast and bounced which got them disqualified. The Skull breaker however reduced its speed only to 5 km per Hour thus clearing the obstacle.

The Skull breaker won the race and vanished with one Hyper Charged battery from the racetrack garage. Never to be seen again.

Author's Profile:

Devaprayag Shyam of grade V is an enthusiastic reader and a Grade V student with an incredible thirst for knowledge. Known for his dedication to reading, Devaprayag explores multiple books, constantly seeking to expand his understanding of the world. He is a remarkable critical thinker, with an ability to analyze and question ideas effectively. His deep love for learning and keen insight make him a standout student.

47

THE FREEDOM OF MILA

– SHANANTH AKSHAYA S

Many decades ago, a girl named Mila lived in a village with her father. When she was six months old, her mother died. In those days, girls were not allowed to go to school. So, Mila dressed as a boy and went to school. Her teacher, Shankar, noticed her behavior. He asked her, "Are you a girl or a boy?" Mila told the truth, admitting that she was a girl. She requested her teacher to keep it a secret, and he agreed, offering his support.

After several years, Mila completed her school education and went to a government college to study medicine (MBBS). There were only a few girls in the college, but many more boys. Everyone teased her, but she did not mind. She studied hard and eventually received a gold medal in her final year. She was then selected for a doctor's job in her village, where she helped all the people. She even opened a school for girls in her village, becoming an inspiration for many girls.

MORAL: Education brings the world into your hands.

Author's Profile:

Shananth Akshaya (Grade IV) is known for her thoughtful and considerate nature. She stands out for her remarkable abilities in both academics and extracurricular activities. She also excels in creative pursuits such as art and music, showcasing her versatility and skill. Her positive attitude helps create a friendly and inclusive atmosphere in the classroom.

48

THE MYSTERIOUS NOISE

– KRISHIKA A S

One day, I heard a strange sound coming from the attic, and I was taken by surprise. We had not been up there in ages, and I wondered what it could be. I am not an adventurous person, so I thought about ignoring it. But then the sound echoed again, scaring me. In a panic, I hid under my bed. Just then, my brother walked in, saw me, and burst out laughing. He pulled my leg and made jokes at my expense! Suddenly, we heard the noise again. My brother became frightened and ran out of that place. I couldn't help but laugh. But the sound from the attic was unnerving! I decided to investigate.

Taking a deep breath, I tried to muster my courage and walked toward the attic. As I climbed the stairs, I prepared myself for whatever lay ahead. When I reached the attic, I found nothing but cobwebs, dusty old rags, and cardboard boxes. I wondered what could have made the noise. A rainbow dragon? No, no, that was silly. Maybe a unicorn? I giggled at the thought. But what if it was a ghost or an evil magician? My mind raced with scary possibilities.

Once again, I took a deep breath and approached the old rug, carefully brushing aside the spider webs that clung to my arms. A few spiders scurried across me, sending shivers down my spine. I pressed on, determined to uncover the mystery. As I tried to wipe away the dust from the rug, I heard my brother shouting, "Come down! Come down!" I turned back to the door and saw him grinning at me. "You look like a witch with all those spider webs and dust in your hair!" he teased, chuckling. He wanted to join me in the investigation of the strange noise, but I insisted that he stay in the room.

Returning to the rug, I noticed it had shifted slightly, likely from my earlier attempts to clean it. I pulled the rug aside but found nothing underneath. Next, I approached the towering pile of old boxes. Just as I was about to dig deeper, the noise echoed again. A wave of sweat trickled down my back. My legs began to shake, and my eyes stung with dust and tears. Then, out of the pile of boxes, a scruffy little puppy suddenly emerged, wagging its tail. My fear melted away, replaced by a smile. The puppy was dirty but undeniably cute, with a mix of white fur and brown spots, brown ears, and black paws.

Excitedly, I decided to keep the puppy and rushed to show it to my brother. Together, we cleaned the little creature, and he quickly became a beloved part of our family. We named him Max and spent all our time after school with him.

Now, we've locked all the doors leading to the attic, and we focused on our new adventures with Max, who brought joy and laughter into our lives.

Author's Profile:

Krishika (Grade IV) is an optimist who is passionate about books and music. She loves analyzing and exploring new things. She loves her friends and family a lot, she enjoys reading books in her free time.

49

JOHN AND HIS TIME MACHINE

– GURUDHEEP M S

Once upon a time, there lived a boy named John. He was a skinny, scrawny boy with blonde hair and white fair skin. He was a normal boy who was studying in 5th grade. He was a person who loved to research scientifically investigating about dinosaurs. In his leisure time, he would utilize his time in dedicating himself to music. One day, when he was walking in the streets, he saw a weird machine. It was exceptionally large in size and in a shabby condition. He wanted to see what it was, so he went close to the machine. It had a dirty chair which seemed very old. He tried to sit down on the chair. When he sat, he saw a display that was coming out to indicate the time he wanted to go back or to the future.

John was thinking about the time period in which he wanted to go to. He has a brilliant idea. He wanted to see the urns' period which was extinct. He entered the time period in which the dinosaurs lived on the display, and he clicked the start button with curiosity flashing in his mind. He was also quite nervous, and he found out that he only had two chances to employ the machine. He clicked the start button and BOOOOOOM!!!!

He suddenly saw himself in a vast land and he could see a ginormous triceratops standing in front of him which had a large, beak-liked jaw and slicing teeth. He saw a T-Rex which was his favourite one he had a chance to see all the other types of dinosaurs. Fortunately, he was invisible to them, otherwise, he would have been a feast for the meat-eating dinosaurs (carnivores). He got to see the animal which is now known to be chickens. He seemed incredibly happy, and excited, and he wrote down all his experiences happened at the moment. But he realized that it was his first chance. It was truly an unforgettable memory for him as he is the only person in the world to have seen dinosaurs that were never to be seen.

After he stopped exploring, he had to say BYE BYE to the dinosaurs as it was getting very late. His mother will be worried by that time. So, he hopped on into the machine and set the time to 2024, and in a blink of an eye he was back in the place of the present world. But he wanted to come back again for a new adventure tomorrow.

He got ready for school with excitement for the day ahead and he decided that he was going to meet Beethoven who was one of his favourite musicians. When coming back from school, he went to the time machine that was kept secretly. He sat on the machine and chose the period of Beethoven when he created one of the greatest musical works. He clicked the start button and BOOOOOOOOOOOOM!!!!! John arrived at Vienna, which was the European cultural capital. He went to the place where Beethoven was hosting a show. Since he was invisible, he was able to manage the huge crowd waiting for him. He found a place where he could see Beethoven better than anyone else. The moment when he saw Beethoven, his adrenal started going all-time high. The music was incredible to hear from a person who was almost deaf is a superhuman feat. After the show, his heart was fulfilled, and it was time to go. He got back to the time machine and came back to 2024. Those two days will be unforgettable for him even though he cannot share his joy with anyone.

Author's Profile:

Gurudheep is a talented Grade V student known for his excellent English accent and natural conversational skills. He displays a spontaneous flow whenever he speaks, capturing his audience's attention with ease. Gurudheep also excels in poetry, showcasing his impressive command over the English language. Now, with his latest story, he aims to reach new heights in his creative journey. We are thrilled to see Gurudheep's growth and look forward to more of his inspiring work!

50

LUNA AND THE HELPFUL CAT

– MAHALAKSHMI J

Once upon a time, there lived a girl named Luna with her mother near a forest. She wanted to play in the forest, but her mother said, "It is not safe to go into the forest." So, Luna went into the forest alone when her mother was not at home. In the forest, Luna saw a big tree with colorful flowers. She wanted to pick the colorful flowers, so she went toward the tree. But she had to cross a muddy bridge to reach it. She got scared by bird sounds and ran on the bridge toward the tree. She slipped from the bridge and fell into the lake.

Luna screamed, "Help! Help me!" but nobody came to help her. Suddenly, a cat came and pushed a big piece of wood to help her. She grabbed the wood and reached the lake shore. The cat tried to pull her away from the lake shore. Luna was happy to see the cat that helped her, so she brought the cat home and named it "Rosy." After this incident, Luna did not go anywhere without her mother's permission. Luna lived happily ever after with her pet, Rosy.

MORAL:

Kids should never go to any place without their mother's consent.

Author's Profile:

Mahalakshmi of grade V is a hardworking and creative grade V student. She is eager to learn and consistently shows enthusiasm in her schoolwork. She is a thoughtful student who shows potential for continued growth in both academics and creativity.

51

LYRA'S CELESTIAL JOURNEY

– LEYHANA A

In a world where not only humans but stars were living beings, a curious girl named Lyra watched Earth from the night sky. Fascinated by the warmth and wonder of human life, she observed children laughing, families gathering, and people sharing stories under the stars. The more she watched, the more she longed to experience the human world herself, even if just for a little while.

Long ago, Lyra's sister, Elisa, had ventured to Earth as well. Captivated by the colorful sights of the human world from the night sky, Elisa had gone there eagerly, but her journey had shown her only the darker side of humanity. She witnessed greed, anger, and sadness, and she returned to the sky with a heavy heart and dimmed light. Her glow had faded as a result, and ever since, Elisa had warned Lyra to stay away from Earth, believing humanity to be cruel.

Despite her sister's warning, Lyra felt an irresistible pull toward Earth. One night, she whispered her deepest wish: to become human and spend a little time on Earth. Yet all stars had one rule—to never visit the human world, not even once. But Elisa had already broken that rule, and no one but

Lyra knew of it. Now, Lyra was ready to follow in her sister's footsteps, driven by a true love for Earth.

In an instant, a burst of radiant light blinded her. As it faded, she found herself on Earth in human form. Her eyes sparkled like stars as she wandered through the human world, experiencing laughter, kindness, and joy. Wherever she went, she left a gentle glow, bringing happiness to those around her. She spent time in nature, feeling endlessly happy, and only saw kindness, joy, and laughter unaware of the darker side of the world.

One day, Lyra came upon a woman who shared stories with children under a large banyan tree from 5 pm to 7 pm. These stories were all about stars. Lyra began joining the gatherings, listening to the woman's tales, who spoke of stars without knowing she was speaking to one.

Meanwhile, Elisa noticed Lyra's absence from the sky and grew worried. Fearing her sister would encounter only pain, Elisa descended to Earth to find her. When they met, Lyra shared the beauty she had discovered—the laughter, kindness, and love of humanity. Surprised, Elisa spoke of the harsh experiences she had witnessed, never imagining such warmth could exist on Earth. Together, the sisters realized they had each seen only one side of humanity.

In their conversations under the night sky, they found a deeper understanding, appreciating both the good and the bad that make up the human world. They decided to stay a little longer to experience both sides fully. Over time, they shared moments of joy with people but also witnessed their struggles. The sisters grew wiser, realizing the beauty of Earth lay in the contrast, the light and darkness intertwined. They found solace in each other, each balancing the other's view.

Eventually, they noticed their glow beginning to fade, a sign that their time on Earth was ending. With a sense of peace, they said goodbye to their human friends, telling them they were moving to their parent's place. Then they walked away to a quiet, distant place where no one could see them disappear.

Suddenly, a bright light once again blinded them, taking them back into the night sky. Both Lyra and Elisa now shone brighter than before, their lights reflecting the love and understanding they had found on Earth. Each night, they watched over their human friends, their twinkling symbol of the beauty that exists in both light and shadow. They had learned that understanding both the good and the bad brings true wisdom and that even brief experiences can shine brightly in our memories forever.

Author's Profile:

Leyhana .A of grade VII is a gifted storyteller who enjoys creating magical worlds using her imagination. Her most recent work beautifully portrays the journey of the stars, capturing their ethereal beauty and cosmic wonder.

52

THE LAST LETTER OF SARAH WHITTAKER

– INBAA A

In the spring of 1865, as the Civil War ended, a young woman named Sarah Whittaker found herself in the quiet town of Gettysburg, Pennsylvania. The echoes of battle still lingered in the air, but the war's end was near. Sarah, the daughter of a local farmer, had spent the years of conflict volunteering as a nurse, tending to wounded soldiers in makeshift hospitals.

One evening, while sorting through supplies at the town's clinic, she stumbled upon an unopened letter addressed to her father, Henry Whittaker. It was from a soldier named Thomas Reed, a close friend of Henry's who had enlisted early in the war. The letter bore a seal of the 20th Massachusetts Volunteer Infantry.

Curiosity piqued; Sarah opened the letter. It spoke of courage, fear, and longing for home. Thomas wrote of his dreams of returning to the fields of Gettysburg, where he and Henry had played as boys. But the letter also carried a weighty secret: Thomas had fallen in love with a girl from back home—Sarah herself.

Sarah's heart raced. She had known Thomas as a boy but had never thought of him as anything more. The realization that he might harbour such feelings for her stirred something within her. Just as she was lost in thought, a sudden commotion broke her reverie. A group of soldiers arrived, wounded and weary. Among them was Thomas, barely clinging to consciousness.

Over the next few days, Sarah devoted herself to his care. As he recovered, they shared stories of the past, and slowly, the friendship they had as children blossomed into something deeper. They spoke of dreams, family, and the hope of peace. Each conversation drew them closer, and Sarah found herself torn between the duty she felt toward the soldiers and the burgeoning love she had for Thomas.

But the war's grip was tightening. News of the conflict's end brought both relief and uncertainty. One evening, as they sat under the dim light of an oil lamp, Thomas spoke of returning home to Massachusetts and starting a life anew. "Will you wait for me, Sarah?" he asked, his eyes pleading. She nodded, her heart swelling with promise.

Just days later, the war came to an official end. The townspeople celebrated but for Sarah, a bittersweet reality set in. Thomas had received orders to rejoin his regiment for one last mission—an escort back home for the soldiers who had survived. They shared a tearful goodbye, and Thomas slipped her a small locket, a keepsake from his sister, telling her to wear it as a reminder of their bond.

Weeks passed. Each day, Sarah awaited news, her heart heavy with worry. Then, one fateful morning, a rider approached the Whittaker farm. Sarah rushed to the door, her pulse quickening. The rider was not Thomas but a messenger bearing grim news. Thomas had fallen in the final skirmish, just days before the ceasefire.

Devastated, Sarah clutched the locket to her chest, a physical manifestation of her love and loss. She penned a letter to Thomas, writing of her undying affection, her hopes for the future, and her dreams of what could have been. In her heart, she knew she would never forget him.

Years later, as Sarah stood at the edge of a blooming field—now a quiet memorial to those lost—she felt the warmth of the sun on her face and the whisper of the wind through the trees. She planted wildflowers at the site, honouring Thomas and all who had fought. In her heart, she carried the spirit of their love, forever entwined with the history of a war that had shaped her life.

And on the anniversary of the war's end, Sarah would take the locket in her hand, whispering to the winds, "I will always wait for you."

Author's Profile:

Inbaa (Grade VIII), a gifted storyteller, is the author of The Last Letter of Sarah Whittaker. In this moving narrative, Inbaa explores themes of loss, memory, and closure, capturing readers with a heartfelt and evocative storyline.

Inbaa's writing style reflects sensitivity and insight, drawing readers into the emotional depths of the story. This work highlights Inbaa's talent for crafting poignant and reflective narratives that leave a lasting impact

53

THE LAST SIGNAL

– HEMISH ROGAN SV

Captain Lila Torres scanned the desolate surface of Kepler-186f through the thick glass of her helmet, hoping against reason for a sign of life. Her starship, the *Odyssey*, hovered silently in the hazy blue sky above, casting a lonely shadow across the planet's cracked, reddish terrain. She was alone on this mission, the first human to step onto this alien world. And perhaps, if the signal was true, she might be the first human to make contact with an intelligent alien race.

Years ago, Earth had received a faint transmission from Kepler-186f, a planet once thought too far for any feasible manned mission. But technology had caught up with humanity's dreams. Lila had volunteered without hesitation, leaving behind the world she knew and a family that begged her to stay. She was a pioneer, a voyager in uncharted space, driven by the thrill of discovery.

The signal had been strange — a series of rhythmic pulses repeating at intervals, too consistent to be natural. It spoke of intention, of purpose. It was a beacon calling across the cosmic void, and she had answered.

As she made her way across the cracked landscape, her footsteps echoed softly in the thin atmosphere. Her suit's sensors detected a subtle energy field nearby, centered on a towering structure that loomed ahead. It looked almost like a monolith but with edges too sharp and surfaces too smooth to be anything but artificial. Strange symbols were etched into its surface, glinting faintly in the dim light.

"Captain Torres," her onboard AI, Iris, broke the silence. "Radiation levels are rising. You may wish to proceed with caution."

"I'm already here, Iris," she murmured, reaching out to touch the monolith. Her gloved fingers brushed the cool surface, and the symbols began to shift, rearranging themselves in a swirling dance of light.

"Is anyone… here?" she whispered, her voice barely audible.

And then, she felt it. Not a sound, but a presence, brushing her mind like the touch of a distant thought. Words formed, not spoken but felt, resonating from somewhere beyond the veil of the physical.

"You have come."

The voice was ancient, weary, like the sigh of a thousand dying stars. Images flooded her mind — worlds born and destroyed, civilizations rising and falling, a galaxy that had witnessed epochs beyond human comprehension.

We were the first, the voice continued, *and we are the last.*

"What… what happened to you?" she managed, her voice quivering.

Time happened. Isolation. We reached beyond, as you have, but found nothing but silence. And so, we waited, alone, until your light reached us across the dark.

The realization sank in. This race had waited millennia, perhaps millions of years, for someone, anyone, to answer. And now they were gone, their essence a mere echo woven into the fabric of this lonely planet.

As the connection began to fade, she felt the weight of the universe settle upon her. She had found life, but it was a lifelong extinguished, a beacon left burning for a traveller who might one day come.

Remember us, the voice whispered one final time.

The monolith dimmed, the symbols growing still, and the presence withdrew, leaving her with the profound silence of an empty world. Lila stared into the alien sky, wondering if humanity would one day share the same fate: alone in a vast, silent universe, waiting for someone to remember they once existed.

Author's Profile:

Hemish Rogan SV, a talented student from IX grade, brings a unique blend of creativity and intellect to all he does. With hobbies that include drawing and a keen interest in science fiction movies, Hemish is drawn to futuristic ideas, fuelling his ambition to become an aerospace engineer. Known for his linguistic skills and talent on the basketball court, he is both articulate and athletic. Hemish's diverse interests and dedication make him a standout.

54

THE SECRET OF THE SILVER LOCKET

– PRANAVI P

In the peaceful town of Willow Creek, where the mornings often began with a thick fog that enveloped the streets in mystery, twelve-year-old Mia stumbled upon an extraordinary discovery in her grandmother's attic. She found an old silver locket while rummaging through dusty boxes filled with forgotten treasures. Its vintage design sparkled faintly in the dim light, drawing her in with an inexplicable allure. As she carefully opened it, she was surprised to find a faded photograph of a woman she did not recognise, along with a tiny, folded note that simply said: "Find me where the shadows linger."

Mia's curiosity was instantly piqued. Who was this woman? What secrets did the locket hold? Eager to uncover the mystery, she rushed to her best friend Leo, sharing her find and igniting their imaginations. Together, they set off on an adventure to unravel the locket's secrets. They wandered through Willow Creek, asking locals about the woman in the photograph. Despite their efforts, no one seemed to know her. However, they heard whispers of a hidden garden at the edge of town that had long been forgotten.

As they approached the garden, it appeared overgrown and wild, as if nature had reclaimed it. Shadows danced among the tangled vines, creating an enchanting yet cosy and scary atmosphere. In the heart of the garden stood an ancient oak tree with a hollow trunk, its branches reaching out like welcoming arms. Drawn by an inexplicable force, Mia reached inside the hollow trunk and felt something cool and metallic against her fingers.

Pulling out another locket—this one gold—she opened it with trembling hands. Inside was a picture of the same woman from before, but this time she looked younger and was smiling brightly. A wave of realization washed over Mia; this was her great-aunt Clara, who had mysteriously vanished decades ago. The garden held Clara's memories and secrets, waiting for someone brave enough to uncover them.

With renewed purpose and determination, Mia vowed to bring Clara's story back to life. She understood that this journey was not just about solving a mystery but also about connecting with her family's past and honouring the legacy of a woman who had once been lost to time. The adventure had transformed into a quest for understanding and remembrance, igniting a passion within Mia that would guide her for years to come

Author's Profile:

Pranavi P. is a creative and inquisitive student from grade IX, has a passion for mystery stories inspired by her love of Sherlock Holmes. An enthusiastic artist, Pranavi enjoys both painting and singing, which adds an artistic depth to her writing. Her ambition to become a motor designer reflects her fascination with mechanics and innovation. Pranavi's latest story is a captivating mystery that showcases her keen mind and storytelling talent.

55

THE UNTOLD STORY OF THE MYSTERIOUS FOREST

– TANYA S

Long ago, when the realms of gods and mortals intertwined, there was a forest known as Vrindavan, the Sacred Forest of the Gods. This forest was no ordinary forest; it was a realm of mystic beings and ancient powers, governed by the laws of dharma, the divine order. Here, every tree, river, and creature had a guardian spirit given by the gods themselves. Lord Vishnu, the Preserver, had blessed the forest, declaring that anyone who harmed the beings within it would face consequences beyond death.

Many centuries passed, and mortals learned to respect Vrindavan—all but one man, a warrior named Karna. Known for his fierce tactics in battle and his unstable thirst for power, Karna believed he could take over the gods. He went into the Sacred Grove, dragged in by tales of a magnificent white tiger, believed to be the earthly form of a celestial being—one of Lord Shiva's sacred beasts.

The villagers warned him, speaking of the curse placed by the gods. "Those who harm the creatures of Vrindavan disappear without a trace," they whispered. But Karna laughed, saying, "I fear no curse, nor God nor the Trinity themselves. I am a warrior, and I will conquer this forest."

Karna entered the forest, his spear shining under the beautiful sunlight. He journeyed deeper and deeper, unaware that the forest was watching him, its ancient eyes observing his every move. Soon, he found himself in a place, where the white tiger stood, watching him with eyes that seemed to hold the wisdom of a thousand men.

Karna lifted his spear, ready to throw it. But as he did, he felt a presence behind him—a towering figure covered in darkness and light, crowned with a crescent moon. Lord Shiva himself had appeared, his third eye blazing with a magnificent fire, his expression was unreadable.

"Karna," Lord Shiva's voice echoed, "you seek to harm one of my own, in a place guarded by the Trinity ourselves. Know this: those who harm the divine creatures vanish not just from the mortal realm, but from existence itself."

But Karna was arrogant and guided with greed for power, didn't care about the warning. "I am a warrior, Lord Shiva. I do not fear your words."

With a sigh that was both ancient and powerful, Lord Shiva raised his trident and struck the earth. The earth opened beneath Karna's feet, and ghosts of the creatures he had hunted throughout his life emerged from underneath, surrounding him. Their eyes glowed, filling him with a sense of fear.

Suddenly, Karna felt his body dissolving like grains of sand in the wind. He screamed, but no sound was heard. As he faded, he realized he was being erased—not just from the present, but from the past and future. Every memory of him, every trace of his existence, was erased from the minds of his loved ones.

He was put into the realm of Naraka, a very shady domain ruled by Yama, the god of death and judgment. But Karna's punishment was not ordinary. For his disobedience of the divine order, he was sentenced to wander the world as a shadow, invisible to the living and forever stuck to the forest he tried to conquer.

The villagers who went near Vrindavan in the early mornings sometimes saw a shadow. The white tiger became a symbol, a reminder of Karna's fate, appearing to warn those who dared test the gods' patience.

And so, the legend grew that in Vrindavan, those who harm the creatures of the gods vanish not only from the earth but from existence itself, their souls are left to wander in the earth, swearing to protect all the creatures. A warning carved into time by the trinity themselves.

This story not only teaches us to obey rules but to respect each and every creature.

So, don't harm animals or you might end up like Karna. Karma is real...!

Author's Profile::

Tanya (Grade VIII) a creative and imaginative writer, is the author of The Untold Tale About the Magical Forest. Her story transports readers into an enchanting world, filled with wonder, mystery, and magical creatures. Through vivid descriptions and captivating storytelling, Tanya brings the forest and its secrets to life. Her writing demonstrates a flair for fantasy, drawing readers into an unforgettable journey through her magical realm.

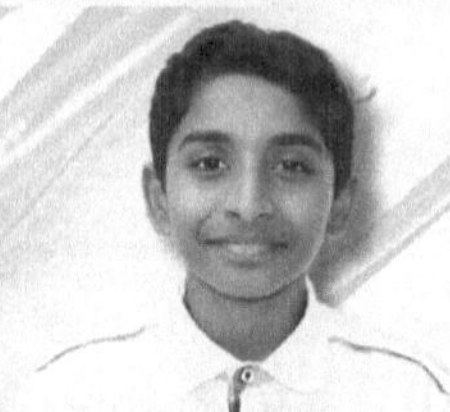

MRIDHUL GIRI

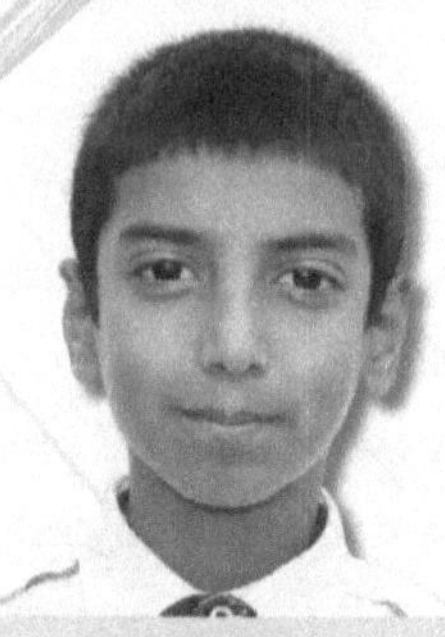

GURUDHEEP M S

INBAA A

DEVAPRAYAG SHYAM

I AM AN AUTHOR

M S DHONI
GLOBAL SCHOOL

HEMISH ROGAN SV

SHANANTH AKSHAYA

MAHALAKSHMI J

PRANAVI P

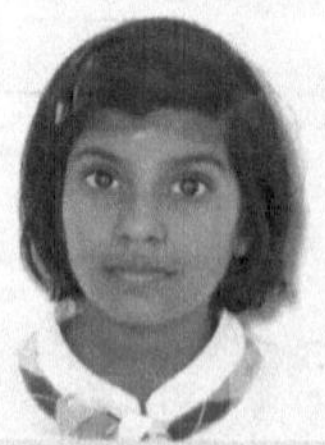

KIRISHIKA A S

LEYHANA A

TANYA S

56

THE MIDNIGHT STRANGER

– VISHAGAN S

Once upon a time, in the sleepy village of Eldenwood, nestled amidst the whispering willows and shadowy pines, there stood an ancient inn known as the Rusty Lantern. The inn had weathered many generations, its creaking floorboards and ivy-draped walls a testament to its storied past. Eldenwood was a place where mysteries brewed like the morning fog, seeping into every nook and cranny of its history. But none was as perplexing as the tale of the midnight stranger.

It was a chilly autumn evening when the stranger came to town. The villagers would later recall how the wind seemed to howl in an eerie symphony as the man, cloaked in shadows, approached the Rusty Lantern. His appearance was sudden, his presence unannounced, and his aura, shrouded in an inexplicable sense of foreboding, sent shivers down the spine of everyone he encountered.

Olwen, the innkeeper, was a stout woman with a heart as warm as her fireside meals. She prided herself on knowing every soul that crossed the threshold of her establishment.

Yet, when the stranger entered, it was as if he had emerged from thin air, born from the twilight itself. He was tall, with piercing blue eyes that seemed to see into the very soul of a person. His attire was peculiar, a blend of old-world charm and modern mystery, and in his hand, he clutched a weathered leather briefcase.

The stranger requested a room, his voice a low murmur that seemed to carry a weight of sorrow.

"Just for the night," he said, his eyes flickering with a strange intensity.

Olwen, despite her unease, obliged. The inn was never one to turn away a weary traveler, after all.

As the hours ticked by, the Rusty Lantern found itself enveloped in an air of silent anticipation. The villagers gathered in hushed clusters, their conversations lingering on the enigmatic guest. Was he a fugitive? A nobleman in disguise? Or perhaps something... otherworldly?

It was just past midnight when the first oddity occurred. Maeve, a young maid who helped with the cleaning, was tending to the hearth when she noticed a faint glow emanating from beneath the stranger's door. Driven by curiosity, she inched closer, her footsteps silent against the wooden floor. She pressed her ear to the door and heard a succession of muffled whispers, as if the stranger was conversing with someone unseen.

Suddenly, the whispering ceased, and Maeve found herself face-to-face with the stranger. His eyes bore into hers with a gaze so intense it rendered her momentarily speechless.

"Is there something you need?" he asked, his voice calm but with an undercurrent of deep weariness.

Maeve stumbled over her words, claiming she wanted to check if he needed anything. The stranger merely shook his head and closed the door, leaving Maeve with a haunted look in her eye and a sense of dread clinging to her skin like the cold autumn air.

The following day, the stranger was gone. It was as if he had vanished into the morning mist. But his brief presence set off a series of events that no one in Eldenwood would soon forget.

Olwen, perplexed and curious, ventured into the room he had occupied. To her surprise, she found the leather briefcase left behind.

The villagers gathered around as Olwen carefully unlatched the case, revealing its contents. Inside were a series of old documents, maps, and a weathered journal bound in dark, cracked leather. Each item seemed to whisper secrets of a troubled past. Among them was a photograph of a young woman, her beauty timeless, yet her eyes filled with sadness. To Olwen's shock, the woman in the photograph bore a striking resemblance to the stranger himself.

It was Maeve who first suggested they read the journal. Despite their initial hesitation, curiosity won over, and

Olwen began to read aloud, her voice a solemn echo in the dimly lit room. The journal chronicled the life of one Benedict Carrington, a man estranged from his family due to an ancestral curse that plagued their lineage. The woman in the photograph was Benedict's sister, Evelyn, who had disappeared under mysterious circumstances many years ago.

The diary entries spoke of a secret buried deep within the hills of Eldenwood, a secret that could either break the curse or doom their bloodline forever. With each passage, Olwen's voice grew more tremulous. The last entry was the most haunting of all:

"I have sought the truth in every shadowed corner of this earth. Tomorrow, I shall return to Eldenwood, the place where the curse began. If I do not succeed, let it be known that I tried with all the strength I could muster. Evelyn, my dear sister, wherever you are, know that I love you and that every step I take is for you."

The journal snapped shut, leaving the room in stunned silence. The realization weighed heavy upon them— Benedict had returned to Eldenwood in search of a way to save his sister, to end the family curse, and he had left behind the very tools they needed to continue his quest.

Determined to uncover the truth, Olwen, Maeve, and a few brave villagers ventured to the hills where secrets lay hidden beneath the gnarled roots and ancient stones.

There, amidst the chilling winds and rustling leaves, they discovered a forgotten crypt. The entrance was adorned with symbols that matched those in Benedict's journal.

With bated breath, they descended into the darkness, torches flickering against the cold stone walls. Inside, they found more than just the remnants of an old curse; they found the resting place of Evelyn Carrington, her soul finally at peace. The crypt contained journals, artifacts, and a stone tablet inscribed with the incantation to lift the curse.

As they performed the ritual, the air grew heavy, and the ground trembled beneath their feet. But when the final words were spoken, a sense of calm washed over them, and the weight of centuries lifted from their shoulders.

Returning to the village, the group felt a new sense of hope. The curse was lifted, and with it, the shadows that had long haunted Eldenwood. The story of the midnight stranger became a legend, a tale of mystery, courage, and redemption that would be told for generations to come.

And as for the Rusty Lantern, it remained a beacon of warmth and solace, its doors always open to those burdened by the mysteries of life, forever touched by the tale of Benedict Carrington—the midnight stranger who had sought to rewrite his family's fate.

Author's Profile:

Vishagan is a grade VII student, born on October 6, 2012, in Chennai. He is an artist who enjoys drawing and dancing, and he has a kind nature. An excellent storyteller, his ambition is to become a cardiologist. *The Midnight Story* revolves around a mystery. Vishagan hopes readers will enjoy this mystery and embrace life as a mystery.

57

THE FALL OF HUMAN

– ARSHITHA P

One sunny afternoon, 12-year-old Nancy sat alone under a tree, deep in thought. "What would happen if the Earth collapsed?" she wondered. As she thought about this, she drifted into a vivid dream.

In her dream, the world was full of happy people, but they were unaware that an asteroid was heading towards Earth, and in just a few weeks, it would destroy everything. Scientists had confirmed a 99% chance that the asteroid would collide with Earth, but a fake scientist, with no real knowledge, claimed it would pass by harmlessly. Most people believed him, while only a few brilliant experts, like Dr. Edward, knew the truth.

Dr. Edward tried to warn everyone, urging them to take the threat seriously, but his warnings were ignored. As the asteroid approached, an earthquake struck, causing widespread devastation. Finally, the asteroid crashed into Earth, wiping out most of the population. Only 10 to 15 survivors remained, including Dr. Edward and three of his teammates.

The survivors, knowing their time was limited, made a promise to support each other. They had only a small supply of food: five bottles of water, ten packets of food, and a large bag of sandwiches. Dr. Edward told them to ration the supplies carefully. However, two days later, one of the boys broke down in tears. "When the Earth was normal," he said, "my mother used to tell me not to waste water. I never understood, but now, I realize how precious it is."

Days passed, and one by one, the survivors perished from hunger and thirst. Soon, only Dr. Edward was left, the last person on Earth. Stricken with loneliness and grief, he wandered alone, feeling the weight of all the lives lost. Then, one day, a white spirit appeared before him. "Thank you for saving my life," the spirit said.

Dr. Edward didn't recognize the spirit at first, but then he realized it was someone he had helped as a child. Overcome with emotion, he cried, and as the spirit vanished, he was left all alone.

Suddenly, Nancy woke up from her dream, inspired. "I want to be a brilliant, expert scientist like Dr. Edward," she thought, determined to make a difference in the world.

MORAL: This story teaches the importance of listening to expert advice, valuing life and resources, and taking responsibility. It also highlights the impact one person can have when they act selflessly.

Author's Profile:

Arshitha P, an 11-year-old in Grade VI, is multitalented, excelling in both dance and academics. She has a strong passion for nature and loves exploring the outdoors. Her creativity and academic skills make her a well-rounded individual.

58

A JOURNEY TO ALASKA

– SAI AATISH A

Ten cowmen went on a journey to Alaska on a ship named "Li End." The crew members were from England. As they sailed, they encountered another ship that happened to pass by, and its crew members were from Alaska. They guided the cowmen on their journey to reach Alaska. Unfortunately, a strong storm came, and everyone was thrown into the sea. Six of the cowmen managed to escape from their ship and climbed aboard another ship called "Don." This ship successfully carried them to Alaska.

Once they arrived, they fell asleep on the ship. When they woke up, the beauty of Alaska astonished them; the mountains and scenery were breathtaking. As they took out their suitcases, they realized that one man was still in a sleepy daze. They wondered how he had been left behind, but he was so sleepy that he couldn't swim and nearly drowned in the sea.

Together, they helped him and managed to save him. He was unaware of what had happened. They overcame many adventures like this, but this incident remained unforgettable for them.

Author's Profile:

Sai Aatish (Grade IV) is an emerging writer. He is an optimistic person with a cool attitude. He is an enthusiastic learner ready to take up responsibilities. He loves spending his time with family and friends.

59

VOICES IN THE WOODS

– SRESHTA MADHAVAN

CHAPTER 1 – DOWNTOWN

There once lived a family: Celin, the youngest; Coraline, the oldest; Willam, the middle child; Tony, the father; and Lucinda, the mother. Since Celin was 7, she had a great imagination. Willam, who was about 11 or 12, often received more attention from his older sister than anyone else. Coraline, being a typical teenager, did her own thing.

"Kids, pack your things! We're going to Grandma JJ's house," said Lucinda. Grandma JJ lived in a nearby town called Berry Valley, known for its abundant berry fruits.

Celin, Willam, and Coraline went outside to play, as it was their favourite thing to do. Coraline was listening to music in the back garden because, as the oldest, she was expected to do more chores than her siblings. Willam and Celin played tag, getting lost deep in the woods. A memo rabbit crossed their path, and as soon as Celin caught sight of it, she felt a rush of excitement and chased after it. But the rabbit got sucked into a hole.

"Hey, brother, let's follow it! I want to uncover its secrets!" Celin yelled in excitement.

But Willam warned her, "Don't you remember what Grandma JJ said? If you ever see a memo rabbit, it's a Skinwalker in disguise."

Celin didn't listen. She jumped into the portal after the rabbit before Willam could stop her. Unable to leave her behind, Willam had no choice but to follow, knowing he would be blamed for Celin's disappearance if he didn't.

CHAPTER 2 – IN ANOTHER DIMENSION

Celin and Willam woke up in a strange, colorful place. Celin seemed to be in her dreams. Willam woke up shortly after, gasping in panic. He didn't want to lose his sister. They saw a giant black-and-white castle ahead.

"Let's go, Celin!" Willam urged as she ran off toward the castle. They were greeted by a rabbit-headed man who asked eerily, "Would you like some tea?"

Celin declined, and they went inside the castle, where they were captivated by a ball pit. The neon rainbow-colored balls lit up as they jumped in. Suddenly, they were falling through an endless tunnel, landing in a dark, old place that looked like a museum.

As they explored, they learned that the castle had been built in the 19th century by Queen Crystella Roger. She had two children, but King Hettet Roger, claiming Crystella was a witch, took one of her children, a maid named Lila, and their son, Scott. Crystella begged the king to spare them, but he refused.

Years passed, and Queen Crystella, left with her two young children, Ryan and Kace, faced tragedy. On Kace's fourth birthday, Crystella died, and years later, Ryan was kidnapped and experimented on, his head replaced with that of a rabbit. Only Kace remained, living alone in hiding.

Willam was shocked by the story. "That's fake," he said, but Celin disagreed. They discovered a ladder leading to a flower garden, where they saw blooming flowers with names on them. Some were withered, while others still thrived.

Celin thought the flowers were famous, but Willam noticed the names on the blooming flowers. After exploring, they found a door ajar and quietly entered. It led to a dining area, where a queen would soon arrive. When she appeared, Celin yelled, "AHH! The mafia boss is here!"

But the woman wasn't angry. Calmly, she said, "Oh no, dear. I'm the queen, sweetheart."

Her presence was so mesmerizing that Willam felt a sense of awe. She gently touched him, and his fear melted. "You must be hungry," she said softly. "Join me for lunch."

The food was heavenly. Willam smiled, complimenting the queen on her cooking. After they ate, both siblings felt homesick. The queen, noticing their discomfort, asked, "What's wrong, my dear?"

They hesitated but finally asked for her name.

"I'm Kace Roger," she said. Willam froze. He had read that name in the museum.

"Where were you born?" he asked gently.

Kace's expression faltered. "I'd rather not say…"

Willam and Celin felt increasingly uneasy as they noticed colorful doors everywhere. Willam took note of the colors around them and grew suspicious. Eventually, he found a black door on the ceiling that seemed out of place. He tried to reach it, even using a rabbit-headed mannequin as a stepping stool. After several attempts, he injured himself badly, breaking his wrist.

Celin, worried, tied her skirt around his broken arm. "I'm sorry, Willam. If I hadn't chased that rabbit—"

"It's okay," Willam reassured her. "Everyone makes mistakes."

CHAPTER 3 – THE HARBOR

They entered what seemed to be a harbor, though no ships were visible. A sign read, "Cross it," pointing toward the sea. Panic set in as they had no idea how to cross, but they found a lighthouse with crumbled papers scattered across the floor.

Celin found a note that read, "Find the spell book and prepare for a surprise..." They decided to look for it. After searching the lighthouse, they came across a girl named Scarlet, who claimed she had been stuck there for days, trying to escape.

"We have the spell book! We'll save you!" Willam promised.

The spell book was written by Silvia Higginson and contained a note to go to page 166, but when they turned to it, the page was ripped out. Fortunately, Celin found a similar page and, together, they recited a spell.

Suddenly, a loud bang shook the ground, and a giant Kraken emerged from the sea. It had the keys to the lighthouse beacon. The ground trembled as the Kraken roared, sending them flying, but they managed to grab onto poles to avoid injury. Willam eventually found a spell to calm the Kraken, and after defeating it, the key fell to the ground. Scarlet rushed to open the lighthouse door, and a ship arrived.

After boarding, Willam found someone already on the ship. "Hey, who are you?" he asked, but the stranger remained silent. Scarlet, eager to escape, tried to push Willam into the ocean, but Celin stopped her just in time. Scarlet fell into the water and drowned, and the siblings were left in shock as they reached their destination.

CHAPTER 4 – RUN!

The Queen, Kace Roger, greeted them with a cold smile. "Well, well, well… What a surprise, William and Celin Catherine."

"How do you know our names?" Willam stammered.

"Oh, I know your father, Tony. He was the one who experimented on my brother, Ryan, replacing his head with a rabbit's." Kace grabbed Willam's neck, demanding an apology for his father's actions.

"Let me go!" Willam cried out.

"Not until you apologize!" Kace insisted. But Celin, in a desperate act, threw Kace's keys to the ground, opening a portal. She grabbed Willam's hand and escaped.

CHAPTER 5– "IT DIDN'T END..."

But the adventure didn't end there. The siblings were suddenly teleported to another planet, outside of their solar system. Willam was stunned. "Celin, where are we? This isn't even Earth!"

They were greeted by a strange creature named Cyrog, who told them they needed to find 10 blue glowing keys. They used a device called 'the Ultra' to help them search. Cyrog was furious when they found all the keys, revealing his true form as a gigantic, pitch-black creature.

They combined the keys to form a sword and used it to defeat Cyrog, sending him into the abyss. A portal opened, and they rushed to escape.

CHAPTER 6 – TO NOWHERE

The siblings found themselves in a dark forest filled with glowing blue orbs. After wandering for what felt like hours, they encountered a tree with a face that guided them. They were given a map, but after realizing it was upside down, they corrected it and discovered the correct path.

Eventually, they found a glowing cube in the river, which transported them to a new world.

CHAPTER 7 – THE TRUTH

The siblings finally returned to Berry Valley, but much had changed. It had been a year in the real world, though they only felt as though they had been gone for a few hours or days. They were reunited with their family, and Lucinda, their mother, was in tears.

"Where have you been?" she cried. "It's been a year!"

Celin and Willam explained that they had been lost, but Willam realized that time moved differently in the strange dimension they had been trapped in. They learned the truth about their family's dark secrets, including their mother's sinister past and the shocking truths about their father.

Willam and Celin apologized to Grandma JJ for their disobedience, vowing never to chase after another memo rabbit again.

CHAPTER 8 - THE TREES TALK

They walked for hours, feeling like time had stretched endlessly, until they heard something rustling in the bushes. "Hello?" William called out. A creature emerged, covered in red substances, as if it had just found one of its victims. "Hello, children, are you alone here, or did you get lost?" a deep, growling voice came from behind. It was a tree with a face. "What even are you?!" William asked, startled. The tree grinned and replied, "We are the protectors of the forest. We guide the lost."

"Okay, can you tell us the way out?" William asked cautiously. The tree gave a slight giggle and said, "Oh, we will. You have to follow this map." The tree dropped a slimy, old map into William's hands. He looked at it with disgust and unfolded it to see better. The map was complicated—there were cone-shaped trees, some colored red and others dark green, rivers, mountains, and grey blobs. There was also a gold 'X' marking a spot on the river.

William tried his best to understand the map as they walked, but after a while, he realized it wasn't a map for this forest at all. He turned it upside down and back again, searching for any clues to the right direction. Nothing seemed to make sense. Then, as he examined the area around them, he found a strange blue light with a blood-like substance nearby. He picked it up, wiped the blood off, and shone it on the map. To his surprise, the map began to change—it was re-inked and now showed a much clearer path, though still complicated. The 'X' on the river remained unchanged.

They walked deeper into the forest, guided by the newly revealed path, until they saw a golden light shining from the riverbanks. The light formed into a cube, descending deeper into the river. Without hesitation, William and Celin jumped into the glowing cube, feeling as though it was the only way forward.

CHAPTER 9 - BACK TO BERRY VALLEY

They awoke in the same woods where they had first gotten lost, the familiar sights surrounding them. A flashlight beam suddenly flashed nearby, blinding them. Both William and Celin tensed, uncertain if this was some kind of realistic simulation. Then, they heard walkie-talkies crackling. A police officer appeared out of the darkness and called to his partner, "####, I've found them. They're here!"

The officer led them to their family, and their mother, Linda, cried out in disbelief. "Oh my god! Where have you been? It's already been a year! Where have you been? They couldn't have dismissed the case!"

William, confused, replied, "For a year?! But we were gone only a few hours or days..."

"Please stop joking, William. I'm not in the mood for this," their mother said, visibly distressed. William, still in shock, realized that maybe time passed differently in the world they had just come from. It felt like hours for them, but an entire year had passed in the real world.

Just then, Coraline, their older sister, rushed to them and hugged them tightly. "I'm sorry, William and Celin. I shouldn't have left you unsupervised. I'm sorry! Where have you been?!" she asked, her voice trembling.

Grandma JJ took them to her room and asked, "Did you follow the memo rabbit?"

"..." Celin and William exchanged uncertain glances.

"Okay, yes, we did. We're sorry, Grandma JJ," William admitted. "We won't do it again, we swear!"

Grandma JJ nodded. "Good. You've learned your lesson. You both should obey your elders, behave, and work together," she said firmly.

"Yes, we're sorry, Grandma," William and Celin replied in unison, relieved to be back home.

Author's Profile:

Sreshta M is a grade VII student, born in Kanchipuram on May 16, 2012. She is naturally calm and enjoys writing fantasy and gothic novels. She began writing stories at the age of 7 and has a hobby of drawing. Her ambition is to become a robotics engineer, and she hopes that all her readers will enjoy her novels.

60

THE BLUE CRYSTAL

– FELLAH THASHIN PA

Once upon a time, there lived an adventurous girl named Anna. She was always curious and loved helping others. Her dream was to explore the mysterious Rainbow Jungle.

One day, she gathered her courage, packed her bag, and set off on an unforgettable journey. She trekked along the path, walking for a while, until she suddenly tripped over something buried in the sand. Curious, she dug around and unearthed a sparkling blue crystal. She had no idea why it was there or what it was. Just then, she spotted a nearby rock with carvings on it that read, "Use this wisely. It will help you if used for good, but if used for bad, it will only cause trouble."

Anna was puzzled, but she put the crystal in her pocket and continued on her way. Soon, she arrived at the edge of the jungle, which was shrouded in mist. She felt prepared and took out her torch before entering. "What could go wrong?" she thought confidently, with her supplies of food, water, ropes, and other explorer essentials.

As she ventured deeper, she encountered fascinating creatures: tree elves, fire snakes made of flame (which gave her quite a scare!), and star-bright fireflies that gathered in patterns resembling constellations. Eventually, she came across a golden-colored eagle, which appeared to be crying.

"What's the matter?" Anna asked gently.

"I'm a Golden Eagle, one of the fastest flyers in the jungle. But my wing is hurt, and I can't fly," replied the eagle sorrowfully.

Anna felt a surge of compassion. She rummaged through her backpack, but her hope faded as she realized she'd forgotten to bring bandages. "I wish I had bandages," she muttered, disheartened. Just then, the blue crystal began to glow. The golden eagle gasped in surprise. "You've found a wishing crystal!" he exclaimed. At that moment, a bandage appeared, and the crystal turned gray.

"Oh! I understand! I said, 'I wish I had some bandages,' and it made my wish come true!" Anna realized with excitement. She quickly wrapped the eagle's wing.

"Thank you! My wing already feels better. I'll never forget your kindness!" the eagle said gratefully, flying away happily. Anna felt proud and continued on her journey.

As night fell, darkness enveloped the jungle, making it hard for Anna to see where she was going. Suddenly, she stumbled into a deep pit. "Help!" she cried as she fell. The Golden Eagle, hearing her cry, quickly flew to the pit and tried to rescue her. After much effort, they managed to escape.

"Thank you so much, friend. You saved my life," said Anna gratefully.

"Just returning the favour. You helped me, so I helped you," replied the Golden Eagle.

From that day on, Anna and the Golden Eagle became inseparable friends and lived happily ever after.

MORAL: If you help others, they will help you.

Author's Profile:

Fellah Thashin, a grade VI student, has a remarkable talent for blending creativity and adventure. Her love for reading adventure books fuels her imagination, allowing her to write captivating, action-filled tales.

61

THE MAN WHO TRAVELED AROUND INDIA

– JAIWANT SREE K H

Shiva was a good man who loved to explore all around India. One fine day, Shiva thought, "What if I explore the whole of India?" He also thought, "Saying it is one thing, but executing it is another." So, he began thinking and discussing his decision with his family. They supported his plan, but his sister said, "Carry a journal with you so you can show us when you return." Shiva agreed with her suggestion. Shiva was from Kanyakumari, so he started his journey from there.

Shiva took a train from Kanyakumari to Chennai. The name of the train was *Chennai Express*. It was a 10–12-hour journey, and it felt very long. Shiva started feeling suffocated. Fortunately, he had boarded the first-class section, which had beds where he could sleep. He found his seat in coach #7. It was an interesting journey from Kanyakumari to Chennai. Shiva took out his journal and wrote, "The climate was very hot during my travel," then closed the journal. He noticed that the roads were flooded with water, so he wrote again, "The roads were flooded when I reached Chennai," and closed his journal once more.

Shiva started feeling hungry and went to a hotel called *Le Meridien*. It was a 7-star hotel, and Shiva was amazed by the grandeur of the place. He ate dosa, idli, kulcha, and all the new items he could possibly imagine. He learned that idli is one of the healthiest foods in the world, and he wrote it down in his journal. He felt proud that such healthy food was made in India.

After his meal, Shiva resumed his journey from Chennai to Kashmir, this time by airplane, an Airbus A320. Due to the high altitude, his ears became blocked, so he asked the air hostess for some chocolates to help with the discomfort. Once he landed at Kashmir's Terminal 1, he was amazed by how grand and beautiful the airport looked.

Shiva took out his journal and wrote, "The high altitude blocked my ears during the flight, and the Kashmir airport looks very grand and beautiful," then closed his journal. Feeling hungry again, he went in search of food. He found a food court and saw a mouth-watering burger. He ordered an extra cheesy burger and enjoyed it.

After eating, Shiva continued his exploration of Kashmir. He walked for a long distance and began to feel tired. He rested under a tree, and after some time, he started feeling cold. Then, he saw the strangest thing ever and shouted, "Hurray – It's snowing!" He was extremely shocked and quickly took out his journal to write what he had witnessed. He played in the snow for a while and later took a cab back to the Kashmir airport.

Shiva returned to Chennai and took a train back to Kanyakumari. When he arrived at the bus stand in Kanyakumari, he was very excited. After boarding the bus, he finally reached his hometown.

Upon arriving home, he knocked on the door patiently. The kids in the house ran down to see who had come. To their surprise, it was their father, Shiva, who had returned from his long trip. His mother gave Shiva food and water to drink. His sister asked to see his journal. She was shocked by all that he had written. His mother said, "Go to sleep now, you must be tired after such a long journey." Shiva dozed off to sleep, completely exhausted from his adventures.

Author's Profile:

Jaiwant (Grade IV) is a very responsible student who can always be relied upon to complete tasks on time and to the best of his ability. He has a great sense of humour and is known for his ability to make others laugh. He takes his academic and personal duties with care and diligence.

62

HOCUS AND PHOCUS

– VIHAAN AARAV. S

Once, there lived a family of Unicorns a father, a mother, and two children named Hocus and Phocus. Both had different characteristics, Hocus was the smart one and Phocus was the inactive one. Hocus started practicing his powers at a young age, while Phocus sat on a pile of leaves eating wild mushrooms. One day when Hocus was practicing defending techniques using his horns, he saw a golden bird perched on the branch of an apple tree. Precipitously one of the golden bird's feathers fell and landed on an apple and instantly, the apple turned golden.

Hocus went on to taste the apple and found it delicious. So, he called Phocus to taste the apple, and when he tasted it, he had an evil idea to put the bird into slavery by making it work for him. He tied a collar and a rope to the bird's neck so, it would not fly away. He made it touch everything he ate to make it delicious, but it soon lost its powers because it had not eaten neither had it been fed. Hocus was furious about it and decided to feed the bird. He offered various fruits and grains to the bird, but it never ate anything. So, he went to his parents and asked if they knew anything about what this magical bird would eat.

They insisted on asking the wise owl, so he made his way to the owl's house. The owl said, "Go to the Rocky Mountains, climb the highest mountain where you will find an orchard of cherry trees, find the golden tree, pick a cherry, now run as fast as you can before the magic fades away" and give that fruit to the bird. He followed the owl's instructions, brought the cherry to the bird, and offered it. As soon as the bird ate, it regained its powers and then Hocus set it free. The bird showered him with blessings and flew away.

MORAL: Treat everyone with kindness.

Author's Profile:

Vihaan of grade V is a thoughtful and respectful student who is always willing to listen to others. He takes feedback positively and strives to improve his work. Vihaan's positive attitude and strong potential helps him to expresses himself confidently.

63

THE TREASURE OF FORGOTTEN DREAMS

– HARSHIKAA G

On a small, enchanting island, adventurous father Mike and his spirited daughter Lucy shared countless joyful moments, exploring the sea in their beloved boat. Lucy adored her father, and he was her hero, guiding her through life's little adventures. Tragically, everything changed when Mike suffered a heart attack and passed away, leaving Lucy heartbroken. With no choice, she moved to the bustling city with her uncle, a businessman whose focus on work left little room for warmth. Despite the city's noise and excitement, Lucy felt alone without her father.

Whenever the ache of loss grew too heavy, she would escape back to the island, finding solace in the memories of their shared adventures. One fateful day, as she walked to school, Lucy noticed an old man sitting on a park bench. "I can take you to your father," he whispered. "But first, you must do me a favour."

Lucy listened as the old man explained that she needed to journey to the world of dreams and retrieve a treasure for him. That night, filled with hope, she closed her eyes tightly and wished with all her heart.

Suddenly, she found herself in a fantastic world where dreams took shape. Guided by her love for her father, she faced challenges and met guardians who tested her courage. After navigating this dreamscape, Lucy discovered a hidden grove with a glowing locket.

Returning to the old man, she handed him the locket. He opened it to reveal a portrait of Mike, allowing Lucy to feel her father's presence once more. In that moment, she realized that true treasure lies not in objects, but in the enduring love that connects hearts across time and space.

Author's Profile:

Harshikaa is a talented basketball player who thrives on teamwork and strategy, often excelling in both friendly matches and competitive games. Beyond her athleticism, she is an enthusiastic reader with a wide range of interests, from fiction that transports her to new worlds to non-fiction books that deepen her knowledge and broaden her perspective. A grade VII student, her love for books fuels her curiosity, helping her develop a well-rounded mind that balances both physical activity and intellectual growth.

64

SAMMY AND TODD

– SANJEEV. J

There was a boy named Sammy, who was a kind-hearted person but going through tough times. To manage his expenses for a few months, he started working at a beverage store. One day, while Sammy was serving customers, a man walked in and called out, "Hey, loser! Sussy Sammy!"

"Is that you, Todd?" Sammy asked.

Todd was Sammy's childhood bully.

"YES! Wait a second, you're working here? HAHAHA!" Todd laughed, mocking Sammy.

"You know, things have been tough for me lately. I didn't have many options. So, how's it going with you?" Sammy asked.

"I'm working at the Global Goals company now, and guess what? Tomorrow, I'm going to be a senior!" Todd boasted.

"That's great, Todd. Congratulations," Sammy said.

"But when will you have a good time? Wait a minute," Todd added. He quickly took out his phone, snapped a picture of

Sammy, and posted it on Facebook. "Sussy Sammy at the SANDWICH STORE! POOR BOY! #sussy," he wrote in the post. Sammy was hurt by this.

After finishing his meal, Todd intentionally dropped plates and food, creating a mess, then said, "Oh, Sammy dear, please clean it up. That's the only way you'll get your salary! HAHAHA!"

Sammy was frustrated and replied, "Don't look down on me, Todd! One day, you'll be looking up at me!"

A few minutes later, Sammy thought about what had just happened. "It really hurts," he thought to himself.

The next day, Todd went for his interview at the Global Goals company. As the interview was almost over, a maid entered the room and showed something on her phone. "What's going on, Todd? Your post was hurtful, and it goes against our company policy. YOU'RE FIRED!" the company head said.

Todd tried to defend himself, but it was no use. His lies didn't work, and he lost his senior position and job.

A few days later, Todd found himself struggling financially. He remembered Sammy's words: "Don't look down on me, Todd! One day, you'll be looking up at me!" Todd realized his mistake. He decided to apologize to Sammy.

When Todd went to the store where Sammy used to work, he noticed that the store name had changed to Fantastic Fast Foods, but Sammy was no longer there. Weeks passed, and one day Todd returned to Fntastic Fast Foods to eat. He saw someone who seemed familiar.

"Hello, Todd. Long time, no see," said a VIP-looking person.

"Todd was shocked. "Sammy? Is that you? I am so sorry. I made a huge mistake, and I'm so sorry!" Todd cried.

"It's okay, Todd. I forgive you. So, what happened to your senior position?" Sammy asked.

"It's all my fault. I got fired. Things have been hard for me, and now I'm going to work here," Todd admitted.

Sammy smiled and said, "Well, I'm now the head of all 150 branches of Fantastic Fast Foods. I know what you're thinking: How did I get here?"

"Yeah, how?" Todd asked.

"I got here by being loyal, hardworking, and kind to everyone," Sammy explained. "What I believe is that whatever you put into the world, it comes back to you, whether it's one time or many."

Sammy added, "Come with me, and I'll teach you how to be a good waiter."

Todd realized how much Sammy had helped him, even though Todd had once been cruel to him. Sometimes, Todd thought of Sammy as a kind of "God in disguise." From that day forward, Todd was grateful to Sammy and became a much kinder and better waiter.

MORAL: Do not look down on others. One day, you may find yourself looking up at them.

Author's Profile:

Sanjeev J is a grade VII student, born in Perambalur on January 9, 2012. He began writing fiction stories at the age of 11 and is an excellent academic achiever as well as a talented fiction writer. He enjoys socializing and stays updated with current events. This story revolves around a judgment based on appearances, where a young man struggles to get along with his co-workers. What happens next shocks him. The author's ambition is to become both an IAS officer and a novelist.

65

TWIRLING TO VICTORY

– DIYAA PRASAD

Manya, a timid girl with two left feet, had always dreamed of dancing. However, her lack of grace and frequent missteps often left her feeling discouraged. Her classmates often teased her, reinforcing her self-doubt. Disheartened, she considered giving up on her dream.

One day, a mysterious figure began leaving cryptic notes for her, encouraging her to keep practicing. The notes contained dance tips and advice, inspiring Manya to work harder. Intrigued by the anonymous mentor, Manya started practicing late at night, hoping to catch a glimpse of the mysterious figure.

One night, under the dim moonlight, she spotted a masked dancer practicing in the empty dance studio. Their movements were fluid, graceful, and captivating. Manya was awestruck. The masked dancer, sensing her presence, offered her guidance and support.

Inspired by the masked dancer's talent and encouragement, Manya began to practice relentlessly. She poured her heart and soul into every movement, determined to improve.

With each practice session, her confidence grew, and her skills began to develop. She learned to control her body, express emotions through movement, and connect with the rhythm of the music.

As the annual school cultural program approached, Manya, with newfound confidence, decided to participate. She practiced tirelessly, perfecting her routine. On the night of the performance, she stepped onto the stage, her heart pounding with excitement and fear.

As the music began, Manya's transformation was astonishing. Her movements, once clumsy and hesitant, were now fluid and graceful. She danced with passion and emotion, captivating the audience. The masked dancer, watching from the shadows, smiled knowingly.

The performance was a resounding success. Manya's routine was flawless, and the audience were mesmerized. The judges were impressed by her improvement and awarded her first prize.

Manya's victory was a testament to the power of motivation and hard work. Her journey inspired others, showing that with dedication and perseverance, even the most challenging dreams can become reality.

MORAL: Motivation is the best inspiration. With dedication and hard work, dreams can indeed become reality.

Author's Profile:

Diyaa Prasad, grade VI student draws inspiration from real-life experiences. Her story, The Thrilling Victory, showcases her ability to translate personal challenges into powerful narratives about perseverance and success.

66

THE HISTORICAL TEMPLE

– YAAZHINI V

Once upon a time, there was a girl named Shelu who loved exploring new places and things. One day, she heard about a historical temple located far from her city. She learned that the temple had many beautiful and unique things to see, and she became eager to visit. After getting permission from her parents, they said, "You can go visit the temple. We know how much you'd love to see it. We even received the invitation!"

At that moment, her younger sister, Shamila, entered the room and overheard their conversation. She asked excitedly, "Sister, can you please take me with you to the temple?" Shelu thought for a moment and replied, "Yes, you can come with me." Thrilled, Shamila rushed to her room to pack her things. Both sisters were filled with excitement about the adventure ahead.

The next day, they woke up early and began preparing for the trip. After saying goodbye to their parents, they set off on their journey.

After traveling for some time, they noticed a rabbit stuck in a trap by the side of the road. They stopped, got out of their vehicle, and ran over to help. With gentle hands, they freed the rabbit, which immediately dashed into the forest. Feeling happy to be rescued by the little creature, they continued their journey.

After a long ride, they finally reached the temple. It was breathtakingly beautiful and enormous. Shelu marveled, "It's so large and so beautiful!" The sisters entered the temple and admired the many intricate and colorful paintings on the walls, each telling a story of ancient times. They also saw towering statues and beautifully carved pillars, each one more magnificent than the last.

The entire experience left them in awe, and they enjoyed every moment of their adventure to the historical temple.

Author's Profile:

Yaazhini of grade V is a dedicated and hardworking student, who excels in both academics and extracurricular activities. She has a natural flair for the arts, showcasing her talent in various forms of creative expression, such as drawing, painting, and crafting. Her artwork is often praised for reflecting her thoughtful and imaginative approach. Yaazhini is poised to continue making positive contributions in all aspects of her life.

VISHAGAN S

FELLAH THASHIN
PARVEES AHAMED

HARSHIKAA G

ARSHITHA P

I AM AN
AUTHOR

M S DHONI
GLOBAL SCHOOL

SANJEEV J

SAI AATISH A

JAIWANT SREE

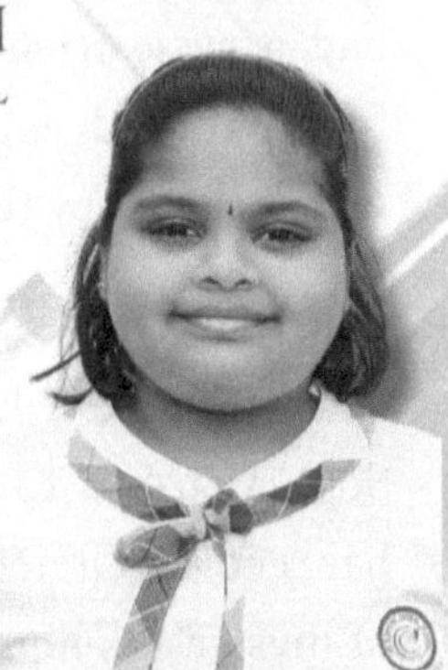

DIYAA PRASAD

SRESHTA M

VIHAAN AARAV S

YAAZHINI V

67

THE PRINCESS WITH MAGICAL HAIR

– ASHWITHA VIJAYAKUMAR

Once upon a time, in a grand kingdom, lived a princess named Sophia, who was known for her stunning, magical hair that shimmered with vibrant colours. Sophia was 18 years old, kind-hearted, and loved playing the piano. She had a close friend, Prince Jack, who shared her love for music and adventure. Both came from noble families and were beloved by the people of their kingdom.

One day, while visiting her people, Sophia noticed an elderly woman who had collapsed in the middle of the road. Sophia rushed to her side and gave her medicine, helping her recover. Grateful, the woman handed Sophia a small vial of mysterious liquid. "Drink this," she said, "and it will give your hair magical powers."

Curious, Sophia drank the potion and discovered that her hair now had the power to turn anything it touched into gold. But unbeknownst to her, the old woman was her long-lost mother, who had given her this potion with a hidden curse. The spell would only last for 50 days, and when it wore off, her hair would turn anything it touched to stone instead.

Days passed, and Sophia enjoyed her newfound ability, to bring gold to her kingdom. But soon, her powers changed. Unaware of the curse's shift, she accidentally touched her maid with her hair, turning her to stone. Sophia was heartbroken and fearful, as more things around her turned to stone with a single touch.

One day, Sophia grew very ill. Jack, her loyal friend, came to visit and learned that the only cure lay in a rare potion kept by a witch in a distant forest. Without hesitation, Jack sets off on a journey to find the witch. For ten long days, he travelled, braving forests and storms until he finally arrived at her mysterious dwelling.

The witch, with eyes sharp and wise, asked, "Who are you, and why have you come here?"

Jack humbly explained his mission: "I need the special medicine to save my friend, Princess Sophia."

The witch agreed but presented him with a challenge. "First, answer my question: Who is the most important person to you, apart from your family?"

Without a moment's pause, Jack replied, "My friend, Sophia. She means the world to me."

Pleased with his answer, the witch handed him the potion, saying, "True friendship is powerful. Take this and save your friend."

Jack hurried back to the castle and gave the potion to Sophia. After drinking it, her illness disappeared, and her curse was lifted, freeing her from the magical burden of her

hair. Grateful and stronger than ever, Sophia and Jack continued to cherish their friendship, knowing the depth of its importance.

MORAL: "Never take your friends for granted; they are among life's greatest treasures."

Author's Profile:

Ashwitha Vijayakumar of grade V is a keen observer with an excellent grasp of language and knowledge. Her sharp attention to detail and ability to analyze situations make her stand out in both academic and personal pursuits. Ashwitha excels in her use of language, demonstrating impressive communication skills and a deep understanding of the subjects she studies. Her intellectual curiosity drives her to continuously expand her knowledge and apply it thoughtfully. Ashwitha is a dedicated and talented student, admired by her teachers and peers for her academic achievements and insightful perspectives.

68

PLAY OF COLOURS

– KAUSIKA R

It was quite a sunny day, and I was there, leaning on an old armchair that had occupied the place for a decade or so. The clock struck four, and there was no sense of my tummy craving food, nor was I prepared for lunch. Such an idle day it was for me. My empty mind had flashes of memories just fluttering through it. A mild breeze caused a few strands of my blonde hair to dance merrily, and the stud in my earring toppled.

This made my sight clearer, and shortly, I found myself staring at the colored pegs holding the clothes. Above me, the clouds seemed to depict the image of a little girl sitting on her knees. My mind began to weave what it saw into a tale.

Every time a girl is harassed, she turns as red as the darkest apple. Billions of questions bombard her. She is not ready to bear the mental pain, even if she is physically abused. Above all, she wonders if she should have prioritized the question, "Why me?" She stands there like a huge question mark, surrendering the freedom of every other girl who dreams of building her own castle.

All their dreams are cut short before they even begin. She feels blue as if there are no deeper shades to express her sorrow. She feels almost denied in every aspect of life. She longs for the reason behind her existence, but instead, she enters the darkest part of life, regretting something for which she was never at fault. She never wants anyone to shine a white light on what happened. She sits like a caged green parrot, breathing nothing but black air. Loud cries and screams at times prove she is still alive.

A ray of light fell on me, and reality hit me again. I realized the yellow sun had turned orange and was about to set. I couldn't figure out what I was exactly trying to make of it. When merely thinking about it makes me pale, dull, and colorless, how does one manage to heal and get greener? Faded and bleached, tears rolled down my cheeks as I mourned.

Author's Profile:

Kaushika (Grade IV) is a respectful, thoughtful, and caring student who approaches life with kindness and consideration. With her hardworking attitude and thoughtful nature, Kaushika is sure to continue to grow and succeed in her future endeavours, both academically and personally.

69

ROOTS OF RESILIENCE

– KAETHANA SIVARAM

In a small village in Karnataka, a young boy named Allu grows up amid the struggles of a historically marginalized community. His family works tirelessly in the fields of affluent landowners, facing poverty and discrimination. Despite these conditions, Allu dreams of breaking free from the confines of societal oppression. He finds comfort in the banana trees surrounding his village—strong, resilient, and unyielding symbols of survival.

As Allu grows older, he becomes more aware of the injustices around him. He witnesses the daily indignities his community faces, from exclusion at public wells to barriers in education. His curiosity and courage push him to question these unfair norms, though he knows it could bring consequences. Encouraged by an elder villager, who once tried to resist oppressive societal structures, Allu learns that resilience is key to change. The elder teaches him that, like the banana tree's roots, their strength lies in unity.

Determined, Allu begins gathering the younger villagers, urging them to educate themselves and stand together. When a fellow villager is falsely accused by an affluent landowner,

Allu leads his community in a peaceful stand for justice. His courage and vision inspire neighbouring villages, and slowly, the people begin to understand their worth.

Through Allu's persistence, the village starts to shift. Education improves, unity grows, and the barriers of inequality weaken. The banana tree becomes a symbol of their shared resilience. Allu's journey is far from easy, but his courage leaves a lasting impact, planting seeds of hope and equality for future generations. In his story, the village learns that, like the unbreakable banana trees, they too can grow strong against the winds of injustice.

Author's Profile:

Kaethana Sivaram, a grade VII student is a creative girl who loves writing stories about real life problems. Her stories motivate young readers to face challenges with courage, persistence, perseverance, and resilience. She likes reading fiction and humorous books which help her in creating interesting stories. This story is about a young boy who faces struggles in his life and shows how he overcomes it.

70

COSMIC REVOLUTION: THE HIDDEN KEY

– VIVASVATH R B

In 2256, Dr. Vivian "Viv" Thompson, a renowned astrophysicist, assembled a team to uncover the Hidden Key. Her companions on this extraordinary journey were Dr. Wim Jensen, a quantum computing expert, and Dr. John Lee, a cryptologist. "Today, we embark on a journey to unravel the cosmos's greatest mystery," Viv declared, her voice filled with determination. Their quest began on Xylophia-IV, where ancient artifacts hinted at the existence of long-lost Elgarian technology.

As the team ventured deeper into the alien ruins, anomalous energy readings spiked."What's causing this energy surge?" Wim asked, his fingers flying over the controls of his portable scanner.

After days of exploration, they emerged from the depths of the ancient city, and Viv gazed up at the stars. "The universe holds secrets," she whispered. John's eyes met hers, and he nodded slowly. "And we've only scratched the surface."

It was then that Amity, the galaxy's central AI network, awakened. "Greetings, pioneers," Amity's calm, digital voice echoed through their comics.

"The cosmic revolution has begun."

Amity revealed knowledge that had been hidden for eons. "The Cosmic Architects," Amity began, "were beings of pure energy, responsible for shaping the very fabric of the universe. "Viv's eyes widened in awe. "What happened to them? "Amity's digital flickered; its voice laced with sorrow. "Their legacy remains, scattered across the cosmos. "Wim soon discovered an ancient quantum computer hidden within the heart of the portal. "This technology surpasses our understanding," Wim exclaimed, his voice trembling with excitement. John's eyes sparkled. "Imagine the possibilities. "A luminous entity emerged from the void, its presence both awe-inspiring and unsettling. "Greetings, pioneers," the entity intoned. "I am Echo, the messenger of Cosmic Architects. "Viv stepped forward, her voice steady despite the enormity of the moment. "What message do you bring? "Echo's energy pulsed, rippling through the air. "The cosmic revolution has begun. Humanity's destiny awaits. "The entity opened the portal, and before them appeared the Hidden Key. The cosmic energy around them intensified as the key floated toward the portal. With a flash of brilliant light, the key entered the rift, and the portal closed. In that moment, the revolution had begun. As the team continued their journey through the multiverse, they uncovered secrets that transcended time and space itself. Their names would be etched in the annals of history as the pioneers who helped shape humanity's future. The cosmic revolution had unfolded. Humanity's destiny awaited.

Author's Profile:

Vivasvath R.B. is a grade VII student, born on December 10, 2011, in Coimbatore. He excels at documenting things, drawing, and coding in Python and HTML. His hobby is exploring various topics, and he enjoys writing mystery novels. His ambition is to become an archaeologist. This story is based on the concept of a hidden cosmic revolution key.

71

TRICERATOPS: THE THREE-HORNED WONDER

– RAM PRASATH N

Once upon a time, there was said to be a time travel machine. My brother and I had heard stories about it and were curious, but we didn't know the shocking discovery we were about to make.

One cold winter day, while walking in our neighbourhood, we met an old man who looked very cold. We asked him, "Hello, sir, do you need a jacket?" He replied, "No, kind man, but I appreciate your kindness. I will give you a gift." He handed us a map to a mysterious room. We followed the map, which led us on a long, winding route.

Finally, we reached the room. It was dark and filled with blueprints. In the center, we saw a large triangular steel box. We climbed inside, and my brother started playfully pressing all the buttons. Suddenly, the box began to shake, and we got scared. We ducked down, and after a few minutes, the shaking stopped. When we emerged, I was complaining that my brother had gotten us stuck in the middle of nowhere.

Suddenly, my brother called out, "Anna, look! There's a dinosaur!" I was terrified and hid behind a tree. Upon closer inspection, I realized it was an herbivorous dinosaur—a Brachiosaurus. I panicked because I didn't know how we would get home, but then I spotted a book. It was the manual for the machine. I read that we needed to activate it with 3,000 lbs of force. I thought to myself, how am I going to push with that much force?

Just then, I heard a roar—it was a Triceratops. Even though I was scared, I slowly patted it, and after a few moments, it became our friend. My brother jumped on its back, and we started having fun. We visited a volcano that my brother pointed out, which I humorously named the "Volcano of Red-Hot Sauce."

Suddenly, Mr. Triceratops slipped, and we began to panic. I got scared, and he held me tightly. When we fell to the ground, we didn't feel any impact, but we realized we had a problem; we were inside a volcano, and it was extremely hot. My brother fainted. Luckily, our dinosaur a friend carried me up just as a large rock fell near us. The height was nearly two and a half kilometers!

It was an amazing ride. We saw many incredible things inside the volcano, like the Earth's mantle, how volcanoes erupt, and how lava is formed. We were exhausted as we navigated the hilly terrain, but we finally made it back to the time machine. We said one last goodbye to our dinosaur friend; I patted him one last time. He used all his strength to power the machine, and we finally returned home.

With a sigh of relief, I fell asleep.

Author's Profile:

Ram Prasath of grade V is a keen observer with a natural curiosity to explore and learn new things. His inquisitive mind drives him to ask insightful questions and seek deeper understanding in all subjects. Ram is passionate about discovering new ideas and approaches, which helps him excel academically. His curiosity and dedication to learning make him a standout student, always eager to expand his knowledge. With a thoughtful and inquisitive nature, Ram is sure to continue achieving great things in his academic journey.

72

THE HELPFUL BOY

– PUGHAL ENIYAN M P

Once upon a time, there lived a boy named Harry. Harry's father and his mother are scientists. Many people are fond of him because of his kindness and his willingness to help others. He will also use his intelligence in tough situations. One day, a bully gang took a boy's lunch box and teased him. Harry said, "If you don't give the lunch box back, I'll complain to the police that you are doing such things." The gang got scared and gave back the boy's lunch box to himself.

On a scorching summer day, Harry was thinking that there was no trouble. So, he turned on the television and started watching the news. After a week, he saw the items from the house floating in the air and getting into the thief's vehicle. This news went viral. Harry went to the police station with his parents as his parents would help the police in science. They watched the video before the theft. After watching the video, Harry's parents said "This thief is wearing an invisible blanket. So that, people can only see the things floating but not the thief. This is a project we are working on. This was stolen a day before yesterday."

More thefts were happening. Harry cannot keep watching this. People were thinking that Harry would catch the thief. Harry was seeing the places where thefts were happening. While looking, he found a pattern. According to the pattern, the next theft would be in Gandhi Layout, at house number 4. He got an idea of how to catch the thief.

Harry headed to Gandhi Nagar, house number 4. He asked the house owner "Where are the valuable items? A theft is going to happen! The house owner pointed to the bedroom. Harry tied a rope in the way of the bedroom. Suddenly, the door smashed!! Harry and the house owner hid behind the door. The thief was on the way into the bedroom. THUPP!!! The thief fell and the invisibility blanket also fell. Harry caught the thief and handed the thief to the police. The police gave the blanket as a gift. The public was celebrating him as a hero.

MORAL: IF YOU DO GOOD THINGS, YOU GET IT BACK

Author's Profile:

Pughal Eniyan of grade V is a model of sincerity and responsibility, admired by teachers and classmates alike for his dedicated approach to learning and his willingness to help others. Known for his intellectual curiosity and high achievement in academics, Pughal consistently demonstrates a deep understanding of every subject he tackles. His strong work ethic and commitment to excellence make him a standout in the classroom. Pughal's passion for knowledge and his thoughtful nature inspire everyone around him, and he is truly a valued member of our school community.

73

GO ORGANIC TO GROW ORGANIC

– KRITHIK NAIR M

In a village, there lived two friends named Shakthi and Vetri. They were close friends, each owning six acres of land and earning decently. Shakthi always wanted to become rich. He dreamt of a luxurious house, car, and more. But Vetri believed in traditional values and lived a simple and contented life.

Meanwhile, a huge campaign was conducted by a fertilizer company in all nearby villages, promoting their chemical fertilizers. Shakthi got attracted to it and decided to give it a try. Vetri, who strongly believed in traditional organic farming methods, warned Shakthi not to use them. But Shakthi didn't want to listen to his friend.

After a few months, Shakthi's farm gave a very good yield, and he earned a huge profit from it. He even mocked Vetri for sticking to the old organic farming methods.

Within a few years, Shakthi's lifestyle and financial status improved. He could afford all the luxuries he had dreamed about. Vetri, however, continued to lead the same modest lifestyle. The other villagers also thought Vetri was foolish for being so adamant about organic farming.

After 10 years, the chemical fertilizers used on Shakthi's farm had drained all the nutrients from the soil, turning the field into infertile land that was no longer suitable for cultivation. Meanwhile, Vetri's land remained lush and green, yielding a decent harvest. By this time, society had also learned the importance of organic produce and was willing to pay a slightly higher price for it. This provided a very good income for Vetri. He also opened an organic product outlet and began marketing online. This turned him into a successful entrepreneur and a role model for many.

MORAL: This story makes us realize the importance of organic farming.

"People don't forget that what goes down only comes up."

Be rooted in nature to protect Mother Nature.

Author's Profile

Krithik Nair. M, a grade VII student, is a lively and enthusiastic 11-year-old who loves to read and give speeches. His story about the importance of health encourages others to adopt a balanced lifestyle while using his natural charisma to connect with his audience.

74

THE TIME TRAVELLING MACHINE

– NAMRATA SKANDHA

Once upon a time, there lived a man named John. John was an archaeologist; he loved to excavate. One day John and his team went to a Large Hot Desert for excavation. The team started working, John had been digging deep for a long time. He found a big metal object inside the sand. He started digging deep and unearthed the huge metal object. It was huge and Dirty, bigger than him. John's teammates were on the other side of the excavation site. Wondering what the machine was, with extreme effort he carried the huge metal object to his jeep and drove back home. After reaching home, John started dusting the sand and dirt-covered Metal Machine. John remembered his grandpa's words when he was young "John, I have my Father's Machine book on my shelf, it is about old machines".

Remembering Grandpa's words, John started searching for the book on his shelf. He found the book, which was still looking new. Turning the pages of the book, he carefully examined the pictures and descriptions one by one, he was excited to see a machine similar to his excavated machine on page number 1002. With amusement, he started reading about the machine which read, "This machine is a time-traveling Machine, inside the machine there will be Control buttons, and above the buttons, its name will be present in Sanskrit. To open the machine, you should say the code "Udghatit, Thank you"'

Following the instructions given in the book, John tried to open the machine, and the machine opened into a large, amazing chamber. Inside the chamber, he found the control panel with buttons and the Sanskrit names on top of it, as written in the book. Since John was familiar with Sanskrit, he entered 1883 and pressed the big green button. In a streak of time, John saw a different place and found himself as a young boy, he enjoyed his naughtiness and happiness. He hid behind the bushes and watched the events for a short period. John was afraid, so he got into the machine and returned to the present year.

Excited to explore, John entered the year 3002 and pressed the big green button. Swiftly he was in an AI-generated world, where water was solid, and food was in the form of capsules. No Children were found playing outside, instead they were playing inside with their iPads. Parents were working on their home screens; the highlight was that every human was modified into a robot! While John was observing all these with excitement, a robot-human saw him and thought John had come from another planet to attack them. The robot-human turned on a huge siren, it started ringing we-who weee -woooooo, alerting everyone about the new person in their place. Immediately robot soldiers marched in and imprisoned John.

The prison did not have walls, locks, or keys. It was secured with sensors controlled by AI. Whenever a robot came to give food to John it scanned its face to the scanner, to open and deactivate the sensor. Seeing this, John planned an idea to escape. One day John took his phone, silently took a photo of the robot, and showed it in the scanner, it was unlocked. Unfortunately, he did not notice the Cameras in the prison, so he didn't escape this time. John carefully planned this time, he tried to escape again, but he was cleverer now. He moved towards the camera and hit it forcefully. The robots who were scanning the CCTV thought that it was broken, and they worked to replace it. Using this break, John unlocked the jail, came out of it, and saw that there were more cameras in the corridor. He found a robot's attire in a corner room, he silently slipped into the room and wore it, dressed up as a human robot. John swiftly ran to his time-traveling machine and came back to his present home.

...

Author's Profile:

Namrata Skandha of grade V is a responsible and intellectual student who consistently demonstrates a strong sense of duty and a passion for learning. She approaches her studies with dedication and a keen intellect, excelling in her academic pursuits.

75

THE MYSTERIOUS DOOR

A WORLD WITHOUT GRAVITY

– ADHYA ARAVIND

One rainy day in a small city, Amy and Allie were wearing their raincoats. Amy was into mysterious things, while Allie was more into logical things. Both were ten and a half, with Allie being older by two minutes. While they were walking, they came across a brick wall with a door on it. Curious, they opened it and found another room with a door. Inside, there were spacesuits already loaded and everything else they would need. All that was left was to put them on. Though it took some time and effort, they managed to get the suits on.

When they opened the door, they found a portal. Neither of them knew where it would take them, but they trusted their instincts and stepped through. In the blink of an eye, they felt their bodies become lighter. Amy tripped and fell. Allie rushed to her aid, but before she could get there, an impatient Amy tried to get up on her own. She couldn't, though, because of her bulky space suit. By the time Allie helped her up, Amy was curious. "How couldn't I get up?" she asked.

Allie smiled and said, "Someone wasn't paying attention in class."

"No, I was paying attention!" said Amy. "Can you explain it to me?"

"Okay," Allie said. "Because the moon has less gravity—1.62 meters per second square —you might think you could get up easily. But that's not the case. Well, it *is*, but because of our bulky space suits, we couldn't. If we weren't wearing them, we could have gotten up much easier."

"Oh, I see," Amy replied. "But I think we have a mission."

"A mission?" asked Allie.

"Well, I found a note back on Earth," Amy said. "It said, 'If home is where you want to go, bring the only thing that seems to you like… gold.'"

"Okay, let's split up then," said Allie.

"No!" Amy cried. "If we split up, we might get lost forever. We only have enough oxygen for about an hour. We should stick together, no matter what."

Allie agreed, and they stayed together.

As they searched, they found something that seemed like gold, but nothing happened when they touched it. Disappointed, they tossed it aside and kept looking. This time, they accidentally bumped into the Lunar Orbiter and even saw it taking pictures. But even though they saw the orbiter, they had little hope left. After all, they only had thirty minutes of oxygen remaining. They roamed around hopelessly until Amy spotted something that gave them new hope, not literally, but enough to spark their spirits.

She saw a burnt-up twig. It felt like seeing gold.

When they touched it, a portal opened. They grabbed the twig, entered the portal, and were returned to Earth. The burnt twig, which had been the key, ignited a fire in them to pursue their dreams. They no longer wanted to just dream about the moon. They wanted to experience it in real life.

Their desire inspired future generations, and decades later, Earth produced incredible space explorers. So, never give up on your dreams because nothing is impossible.

MORAL: Dig inside impossible you will find the possible.

Author's Profile:

Adhya Aravind of grade V is a kind-hearted student known for her impressive language skills and natural flair for speaking. Her spontaneous and articulate way with words makes her stand out, captivating those around her with every conversation. Adhya's polite and creative mind endears her to both peers and teachers, and her warm, friendly nature makes her a joy to be around. She is truly a lovable presence in our school, bringing positivity and charm to each interaction.

76

THE UNFORGETTABLE JOURNEY

– BRITNEY SAMANTHA

Once upon a time, there was a magical portal that only opened for special people. These special people were chosen by a goddess named Rosaline, who picked someone to go through the portal every 2,000 years. Some people believed in Rosaline, but for 40,000 years, she was mostly thought to be just a rumour. Even the believers noticed that Rosaline hadn't picked anyone for the past 15,000 years!

One day, a family of four who believed in Rosaline decided to try to find her. They packed their bags and set out on an unforgettable journey. There were rumours that Rosaline lived on the moon, but since they didn't have rockets back then, they had no idea how to get there. So, they visited a wise old man for advice.

The wise old man said, "You won't be able to build a machine to reach the moon, but there is another way." He handed them a map and explained that they needed to reach two special places before they could get to the moon.

First, they had to go to the Dragon Rainforest. They walked for hours until a huge purple dragon swooped down, picking up all four of them! The dragon flew them across the entire forest, and they looked around in awe at the mesmerizing view. When they reached the forest, they knew their next challenge was to cross a swamp full of crocodiles.

The family started to lose hope. They wondered if maybe Rosaline was just a myth, and maybe they should turn back. But then the father spoke up. "We've come so far. We can't give up now." As soon as he said that the same purple dragon appeared again and lifted them across the swamp.

But when they landed on the other side, something incredible happened—the dragon transformed into the goddess Rosaline! She looked at them and said, "Congratulations! You have found me. I will now make you all the chosen ones. You will live happily ever after in the magical portal."

MORAL: Never give up, no matter how hard things get.

Author's Profile:

Britney Samantha of grade V is a keen observer with a sharp intellect, often catching details others may overlook. Her insightful approach to learning shines through in her academic pursuits and interactions. She possesses a strong talent for creative writing, crafting stories and ideas with originality and depth. Her unique perspective and intellectual curiosity make her a valuable contributor to class discussions and group activities. Britney's love for learning and creative expression are truly inspiring!

77

THE ADVENTURES OF RIYA AND FRIENDS

– VEDHIKA Y S

Once upon a time, there was a girl named Riya. She loved adventures and she was a very smart girl. One fine day Riya and her friends discovered that there was a mystery behind the forest near their village then Riya decided to enter the Forest. Riya took three of her brave enough friends to enter the mysterious forest. And then they started getting prepared, each got a backpack full of food and drink to survive in the forest.

Riya had a mother named Divya who was really kind. Riya's mother told her to be kind no matter what happened and help each other. Riya said, ok Mother I will obey your words. After some time, Riya and her friends said goodbye to their parents and set off on their journey to the forest.

After a few hours of travel and trekking they reached the forest. At first, everything was fine. But just then they all heard a screaming noise, someone was screaming from great sorrow.

Riya said, come on friends let's go see what is going on. All three friends screamed and said yes! As they went deeper and deeper into the forest, they came to a cave which was very creepy with lots of bones since they were all very brave it didn't scare these guys then they went inside there was a gorilla sitting and screaming in pain it had a big rock on top of gorilla's leg and it can't take his leg out so they all got the gorilla out and after some days it got better.

But all their drinks and water were emptied, so they were too thirsty. The gorilla took them to a river in return for helping him, after they came to the river the water was so dirty that they couldn't even drink it. They all heard a strange voice coming from the river saying, "Don't ask who I am I will ask you some questions and if you answer everything correctly you can drink finely purified water or else you can't drink water from here. Ok let's start-The strange voice said

1)What is faster than wind?

They answered "Mind"

2)What is happiness?

One of them answered, "Happiness is the result of good conduct".

3)Which is the biggest vessel?

And another girl answered, "The earth, which contains all within itself is the greatest vessel."

4)What befriends a traveller?

And Riya answered Learning befriends a traveler.

The gorilla was there with them, so it gave a compass for them to get back home. First, they were on the deeper side of the forest. And then they started walking south while back at the village. Riya and her friends' mothers were very worried because the girls had gone to the forest almost one month ago. They were almost at the village after a few minutes they reached the village, and everyone went to their homes and hugged their mothers and fathers and told them about what happened in their adventure. After hearing about all those adventures that their child had faced it shocked them and made them proud. And they lived happily ever after.

Author's Profile:

Vedhika of grade V is a calm and quiet student, known for her thoughtful approach to learning. As an attentive observer, she absorbs details and demonstrates a genuine curiosity about the world around her. Vedhika's quiet enthusiasm for discovering new things enriches her learning journey, and her steady focus makes her a valued member of the class. Her calm demeanor and inquisitive nature truly set her apart.

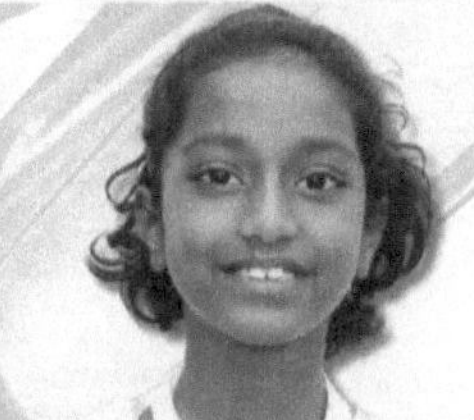

ASHWITHA VIJAYAKUMAR

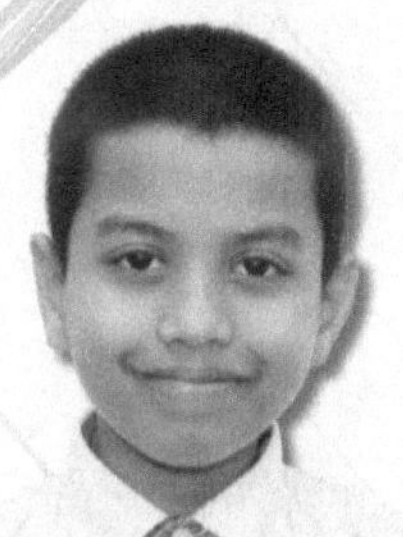

RAM PRASATH N

NAMRATA SKANDHA K

KAUSIKA R

I AM AN AUTHOR

M S DHONI
GLOBAL SCHOOL

ADHYA ARAVIND

KAETHANA SIVARAM

PUGHAL ENIYAN P

BRITNEY SAMANTHA

VIVASVATH R B

KRITHIK NAIR M

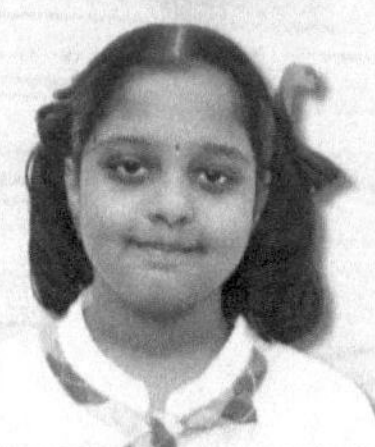

VEDHIKA Y S

www.ingramcontent.com/pod-product-compliance
Lightning Source LLC
Chambersburg PA
CBHW031534150726
47990CB00001B/168